Confidentially YOURS

Heather's Crush Catastrophe

3

JO WHITTEMORE

Confidentially

YOURS

Heather's Crush Catastrophe

3

HARPER

An Imprint of HarperCollinsPublishers

Library of Congress Control Number:
2015943564
ISBN 978-0-06-235897-4

Typography by Kate J. Engbring
16 17 18 19 20 OPM 10 9 8 7 6 5 4 3 2 1

First Edition

For my LoD girls,
and their never-ending support and love

Contents

Confidentially YOURS

Heather's Crush Catastrophe

3

CHAPTER

1

Stealing Ever After

One deep breath.

It's what my *bubbe*, my grandmother, tells me to take whenever we switch yoga poses. It's what my choir instructor tells us to take before we switch from verse to chorus. And it was what I took when the guy at the concession stand handed me my popcorn.

Warm, buttery goodness in a crinkly paper bag.

"Thank you!" I said, breathing deeply again. "And refills are free?"

"If you bring back the empty bag," he said with a smile. "But you don't look like a girl who could finish a Super Popper by herself."

Poor man. He had no idea.

Sure, I'm only twelve and small enough that strong winds send me sideways, but I also have the appetite of an elephant. Last November, I placed third in a pie-eating contest at the Berryville Fall Into Winter festival, and once, my best friend Brooke challenged me to eat a pizza by myself. Not only did I eat every slice, but I also washed it down with a liter bottle of soda.

"You might want to pop some more," I told the guy with a confident grin. "I'll be back."

I walked off to find my friends and was already a third of the way through my popcorn when I found Brooke and our other bestie, Vanessa, at a claw machine.

"Go left. Left," Vanessa was instructing Brooke. "No, your other left."

"That would be my right," said Brooke, brow furrowed in concentration. "And I don't want the pink bear with the crazy eye. I want the blue bunny with the stained paw."

"Why do you want *any* of these?" I asked, wrinkling my nose.

"It's not for me; it's for Hammie," said Brooke.

Hammie was her cat, named after Brooke's favorite soccer player, Mia Hamm. Brooke was big into soccer, and captain and star forward for her traveling soccer team, the Berryville Strikers.

Brooke pushed the button to drop the claw, and it clamped around one of the bunny's ears, dragging it toward the prize chute.

"Woo-hoo!" cheered Vanessa, clapping her hands.

Right before it reached the chute, the bunny slipped from the claw's grasp, back into the pile of stuffed animals.

Vanessa froze with her hands midclap. "Okay, that wasn't me."

Poor V's a little clumsy and accident-prone. If something spontaneously catches fire, chances are pretty good she's around.

Brooke glanced from the retreating claw to the fallen bunny. "Aww, missed it by a hare." She grinned at me. "Get it, Heather? Hare? Hair?"

"You are the queen of comedy," I said with a good-natured eye roll. "Now, come on." I bumped her arm. "We need to get our seats before we're stuck in the front. I don't want to stare up the actors' noses."

Brooke made a face. "It's not too late to change our minds and see *Angry Dead 2*."

"Uh . . . hard pass," said Vanessa. "No blood and gore for me."

"Besides, we all agreed that it was my turn to pick the movie, and I stand by my choice." I crossed my arms and gave a solid nod of my head.

Every Saturday night Brooke, Vanessa, and I got together for movies at my house. We called them Musketeer Movies, since our nickname through elementary had been the Three Musketeers. But for once, I wanted to switch things up and see a movie in an actual theater, one I'd been waiting for all year: *Stealing Ever After*.

It was the story of an evil queen who stole Cinderella's glass slipper, Snow White's poisoned apple, Sleeping Beauty's needle . . . all the things that led to the princesses getting their happy ever afters. The girls then had to fight to get them back. I thought it was a cute idea, but clearly, not everyone shared my enthusiasm.

"Come on," said Brooke. "You know I'm not a fairy-tale romance kind of girl. If it involves a ball, I want it to be a soccer ball."

"Just give it a chance," I said. "It's a movie with girl power. You like girl power!"

"*Angry Dead 2* is a movie with girl power,"

she informed me. "And the star is a redhead." She shook her own auburn ponytail at me for emphasis. "How many redheaded princesses are in *Stealing Ever After*?"

"That's a weak argument," said Vanessa.

"You're only on her side because you like the costumes," Brooke huffed.

Vanessa is obsessed with fashion and makeup and will no doubt be a famous designer someday. Her friend Katie Kestler is always trying to convince her to "build her brand," but I think V is happy just giving style advice for our school newspaper, the *Lincoln Log*. In fact, all three of us write for the advice column, "Lincoln's Letters," along with our friend Tim Antonides.

It was Brooke's idea when our adviser, Mrs. Higginbotham, was looking for something to fill a blank space on the horoscope page. Brooke suggested she could answer questions about sports and fitness, Vanessa could give advice on style, and I could give advice on friendship and relationships. Tim was a last-minute add, with the male perspective on life, and so far, "Lincoln's Letters" has been a pretty popular column.

I hooked my arm through Brooke's. "I promise you'll love it."

"And if I don't?"

"We'll ask Santa to bring you a heart for Christmas."

"Aren't you Jewish?" V asked me, grinning. "Santa doesn't even exist to you."

"Of course he exists," I said. "Who else gives me candy canes at the mall?"

The three of us found seats while the theater's preshow played.

"I object to you saying I don't have a heart," said Brooke, propping her sneakers on the seat in front of her. "I asked Abel to the Fall Into Winter dance. That's pretty romantic."

Abel Hart was her boyfriend, a seventh

grader who was our age but so smart he was allowed to skip sixth grade. He even started his own club, the Young Sherlocks, which Brooke was a member of. It was actually how they'd met.

"You only asked him after he said, 'Hey, Brooke, are you going to ask me to the dance?'" I pointed out.

Vanessa snorted. "*And* you asked him while you had a mouth full of powdered doughnut."

"It was like watching a tiny blizzard," I recalled.

"Give me a break," Brooke said, ripping open her package of candy. "I'm not used to asking."

On top of being the first one we'd ever attend, the Fall Into Winter dance required the girls to ask the guys. I would rather watch *Angry Dead* 2.

"Are you going to invite Gil?" Brooke asked Vanessa.

Gil Pendleton was another seventh grader and the guy we shared our space with at the newspaper. He wrote the horoscopes and was also the assistant photographer. In fact, it was how he and Vanessa connected, when she convinced him to enter some of his photography in a local contest . . . and someone actually bought it!

"I was thinking about asking," Vanessa said with a smile and a giggle.

Then she and Brooke both turned to me.

"Popcorn?" I held out the bag.

"Don't play dumb," said Brooke, taking some popcorn, anyway. "Are you going to ask Stefan?"

Stefan Marshall was this dreamy eighth grader who worked at the *Lincoln Log* as the lead photographer and sportswriter.

"Oh, I couldn't," I said. "He's an eighth grader, and I'm a sixth grader."

"That's only two years apart," argued Vanessa.

"He's a swimmer, and I'm in choir," I tried again.

"Both require lots of lung power," pointed out Brooke.

I stared at her. "Yes. Imagine all the exciting conversations we could have about breathing."

"At the dance!" She held her arms open. "That's what I'm saying. You should ask him."

"I'm sure he's got tons of girls in line." The theater lights dimmed, and I settled back in my seat. "Look, the movie's about to start. Shhh."

"This conversation isn't over," Brooke whispered to me. "You have a big heart and you shouldn't be afraid to use it."

The film began, and for the next two hours, the three of us sat mesmerized, watching the princesses battle ogres and swamp monsters and fire-breathing dragons to get what they most wanted: their happy ever afters.

It was so good, I didn't even get up to refill my popcorn.

When the final credits rolled, all three of us stayed in our seats.

"I want to see who designed the costumes," said Vanessa.

"I want to see if there's more at the end," I said.

"I want to see it again," said Brooke.

But after a while the cleaning crew came through and kicked us out so they could prep the theater for the next show, and Brooke's mom was coming to pick us up, anyway. When we walked to the lobby, I could see that the next show was already sold out.

"Heather." Brooke stood in front of me while we waited for our ride. "I must apologize directly to your face. That movie was amazing."

"It was, wasn't it?" I agreed. "What was your favorite part?"

"When they fought the dragon," she said. "I

know it was all computer effects, but the way Snow White looked that beast in the eye before driving a dwarf's pickax through it . . ." She shivered. "Chills! I have chills!"

Vanessa clutched Brooke's arm. "What about their costumes for the swamp scene? I love how the fairy of the bog sprinkled them with bioluminescent dust so they glowed in the dark." She thought to herself. "I wonder if I could do that with my clothes."

"'You should ask the man with the mustache,'" I said, quoting from the movie.

"'He always knows!'" Brooke and Vanessa chimed in, laughing.

We talked about our favorite scenes the whole ride back to our part of town and agreed to make it the following week's Musketeer Movie too. I had to say I was pretty proud of myself.

When I got home, my *bubbe* was in the front

sitting room, drinking coffee and doing a cross-word.

"Hey!" I said, hanging up my coat.

"Hello, cupcake," she greeted me. "How was the movie?"

"Awesome," I said, bending over to kiss her on the cheek. "Even Brooke loved it, so that should tell you something."

She chuckled to herself. "Brooke puts on a tough-girl act, but I know she's a softie inside. You want some coffee? It's decaf."

It's always decaf since her heart isn't in the best shape, but she announces the fact in case someone thinks she's gone rogue. My mom's a nurse and watches everything Bubbe eats and drinks.

"Thanks, but I'll pass," I said. "Be back in a bit!"

I left her to her crossword and wandered into the living room.

My parents were watching a superhero movie with my big brother Isaac. He's a sophomore in high school. I have an even older brother named Max, but he's away at college and only comes down for the holidays and our annual Halloween party.

I flopped down on the couch next to Mom, and she gave me a squeeze. "How was *Stealing Ever After?*"

"Amazing," I said. "We're going to see it again next weekend. We would've seen it twice in a row, but the tickets were sold out."

"That popular, huh?" asked Daddy. "Martin should be happy."

Martin Hess owned the movie theater and was one of Daddy's clients. My dad's an accountant and keeps the books for some of the biggest businesses in town. My mom is always trying to talk him into moving his business to Chicago, which is maybe twenty minutes away, but

Daddy always reminds her that they didn't leave New York to move right back into a big city.

There was an explosion on the screen, and Mom tapped my leg. "Speaking of which, did you eat something with the girls?"

My mom's brain has the weirdest thought triggers. She can be brushing her hair and say, "Speaking of which, did you know dogs can't see color?"

I smiled at Mom. "How does an exploding van make you wonder if I had dinner?"

She shrugged. "One of the tires went through a restaurant window."

I giggled. "Well, yes, I ate."

"More than just popcorn?" She raised an eyebrow.

"Popcorn and an all-beef hot dog," I said.

"I'm not sure if anyone noticed," said Isaac from the floor, "but we're trying to watch a movie."

"Okay, okay," I said, getting up. "I'd hate for you to miss an explosion." I pretended to step on his stomach, and he grabbed my foot, tickling the bottom.

"Stop!" I squealed, laughing and hopping on my other foot.

"Only if you make me some popcorn."

"Yes! You win!"

He let me go.

"Ooh, popcorn sounds good," said Daddy. "I'll take some too, please."

"You know the microwave kind isn't as good as the theater kind," I teased, heading for the kitchen.

"Would you be a dear and make sure Bubbe takes her evening pills while you're at it?" Mom called after me.

I put a bag of popcorn in the microwave, grabbed my grandma's pills, and opened the fridge to get myself a soda. There was a Fall Into

Winter flyer stuck to the door. All around the borders were reasons to attend:

Food! Prizes! Dancing!

I carried my soda and the pills into the sitting room, and Bubbe made a face but downed them with a gulp of coffee.

"Bubbe"—I sat beside her—"do you think people get what they want if they want it bad enough?"

She nodded. "Of course! If it's meant to be."

I frowned. "Well, how do you know *that*?"

"The signs." She tapped the side of her nose. "You have to keep your eyes and ears open for the signs."

So I did.

On Sunday at synagogue, the director of the community center choir asked if I'd consider doing a solo for the elders, but that wasn't a sign; she asked me that every weekend. I always turned her down, though, because I wasn't a solo act. On Sunday afternoon, Vanessa asked me to go to the Lincoln Park Zoo with her mom and little brother, but that wasn't a sign; her brother had become obsessed with monkeys, especially the fluffy ones.

Even so, I watched and listened for a sign.

Nothing.

Then Monday morning came, and I was standing with my friends in the courtyard outside Abraham Lincoln Middle School. Brooke, Heather, and I were gushing to Tim about *Stealing Ever After*, trying to talk him into seeing it with us.

"I'll buy you some popcorn," I told him.

"I'll win you a toy out of the claw machine," said Brooke.

"I'll help you pick out what to wear for the Fall Into Winter dance," said Vanessa.

I gave her a quick look. She'd mentioned the

dance! Could it be a sign?

Tim smirked. "I don't want popcorn, I don't want a stuffed nightmare from the reject bin at Santa's workshop, and please"—he gestured to himself—"you really think I need help in the fashion department? My look is flawless."

As much as Brooke, Vanessa, and I hated to agree, Tim was a tall, good-looking guy with strong Greek features. He knew it, we knew it, and all his fangirls knew it. Which was why we tried to downplay it as much as possible.

"Thanks for the invite," he said, "but I don't want to see some mushy fairy tale."

"It's not mushy," said Brooke. "It's action-packed and a thrill-a-minute!"

Tim looked at me. "What did you do to her?"

"It *is* action-packed," I told him. "And I guarantee every girl in school has seen it."

At that moment, Stefan walked by with some of his friends, and I distinctly heard him say, "Oh, it was a great movie. But you should ask the man with the mustache. He always knows!"

Stefan's friends laughed.

"See?" Vanessa pointed at them. "That's a quote from the movie. Even Stefan's seen it!"

Tim shrugged like it was no big deal, but I felt like singing.

Vanessa had brought up Fall Into Winter.

Stefan had seen *Stealing Ever After*.

My favorite guy and my favorite movie.

There were my signs.

I was meant to ask Stefan Marshall to the dance.

CHAPTER

2

Thinking of a Master Plan

There was just one problem. I might have been great at giving friendship and relationship advice, but when it came to putting my own words into action . . . that was a little harder.

I couldn't just go up to Stefan and ask him to the dance. If he turned me down, I'd die whenever I saw him, which would be every single day in Journalism. First, I had to make sure he felt the same way about me. But how?

It was a question I wondered about during lunch with my three best friends. They were arguing over who had the best turkey call, another contest at the Fall Into Winter festival.

"Listen, listen," said Tim, tugging on the skin of his throat and warbling.

Vanessa choked on her soda, and Brooke started giggling. Soon, Tim's turkey call turned into turkey laughter.

I gave him a thumbs-up. "You'll definitely take first place in the sick turkey category."

Vanessa and Brooke laughed harder.

"Let's see you try," said Tim, nodding at me.

"Oh, I'm sorry," I said. "My imitations are limited to unicorns and mermaids."

"What's a unicorn sound like?" asked V with a grin.

I cleared my throat, pretended to focus, and sat quietly. After a second, I looked at her. "Not bad, right?"

"You didn't make a sound!"

"And neither do unicorns," I said, smiling at her. "Because they don't exist."

Tim snickered, and Brooke gasped. "You just broke six-year-old Vanessa's heart."

Vanessa wiped away a fake tear. "How could you be so cruel?"

"Uh-oh. Speaking of cruel"—Tim sat up straighter—"here comes Mary Patrick."

The rest of us straightened up too.

Mary Patrick Stephens was editor in chief of the *Lincoln Log* and, to put it nicely, a bit of a ruthless dictator. She carried a buzzer that she beeped at people in the newsroom any time she disapproved of their ideas. Which was often.

Normally, she saved her criticism for the newsroom, so if she was hunting us down in our free time, this had to be something big. I looked at Brooke, and we both leaned sideways to retrieve our book bags. Ever since we'd learned of Mary Patrick's weakness for chocolate, we always kept a safety stash with us. Music soothed the savage beast, and Reese's soothed the savage editor.

But when Mary Patrick finally reached our table, she greeted us with a cheery "Hey, advice team!"

Brooke regarded her with suspicion. "What's going on? Your frown is curving up at the corners."

Tim elbowed her. "I think that's a smile."

Mary Patrick rolled her eyes. "Are you done?"

They grinned at each other, and Brooke rolled a peanut butter cup toward Mary Patrick.

"What's up?" she asked.

Mary Patrick snatched up the chocolate and unwrapped it with a flick of her fingers.

"That's scarily impressive," said Vanessa.

"I've come to ask a favor," said Mary Patrick. "I know some of you have busy schedules, but since the Thanksgiving issue is coming out soon, I need a little more than the usual advice column."

"Like what?" I asked.

"We're trying to emphasize giving back to the community," she said, "so I was hoping you four could write a special advice feature on ways to give back." She paused and stared skyward, as if the next words were difficult. "People really enjoy your column, and I think you could convince them to take action."

Mary Patrick has tried to have our column canceled more than once, so I knew the confession was paining her. I nudged a few Reese's her way, and she immediately pounced.

"A special feature?" Brooke's eyebrows shot up. "Does that mean we get a full-page spread?"

"In addition to your usual advice column, yes," said Mary Patrick with a nod. "But there's a catch: I'd like the four of you to actually volunteer for the ways that you suggest." She fixed her gaze on Brooke. "Which could take up a lot of your time."

A few weeks after school started, Brooke had

gone to Mary Patrick, asking to quit the paper because she'd taken on too many activities.

But now she just smiled at Mary Patrick. "Actually, soccer is done for the season, so I've got all the time in the world." She crossed her arms behind her head.

"Let's not get carried away," said Mary Patrick. "If memory serves, you're still the section lead for your column, and aren't you also in some little mystery club?"

"Young Sherlocks!" Brooke corrected her, leaning forward. "And it's not little. It's just very exclusive."

Mary Patrick didn't look impressed. "What about the rest of you?"

"Katie's been helping me make costumes for drama club, so I'm good to go," said Vanessa.

"I only have Hebrew school twice a week and choir in the mornings. Model United Nations is usually during homeroom," I said.

"I'll see if I can make time," said Tim. "I've got hockey, Greek school, and Greek—" He froze. "Uh . . . yogurt."

The rest of us gave him strange looks.

"Huh?" Brooke wrinkled her forehead.

"The food of my people," he said with a weird laugh.

Mary Patrick shook her head. "So can you guys do this or not?"

"Sure," said Brooke, looking around at the rest of us to make sure we agreed. V, Tim, and I nodded.

"Great!" Mary Patrick scooped up some more Reese's and filled her pockets. "I'll let Mrs. H know that we're excited to get to work."

"Wait . . . 'we'?" asked Vanessa, but Mary Patrick was already hurrying away, back pockets bulging.

"I hope she remembers to take those out before she sits down," I said.

"Never mind that," said Vanessa. "What do you think she meant by 'we'?"

"Probably that she'll be following us around with a buzzer while *we* work." Brooke made a face. "But more importantly, Tim"—she swiveled in her seat—"Greek yogurt is a big part of your schedule?"

He shrugged. "Eating it keeps me busy. Later!" He picked up his lunch bag and then trotted off.

Brooke watched him leave. "What's with him?"

"Maybe today's yogurt was about to expire," guessed Vanessa.

"Or maybe 'Greek yogurt' is code for something else." Brooke narrowed her eyes shrewdly.

"Or *maybe* you should just leave it alone." I pinched her arm. "If Tim wanted us to know, he'd tell us."

She nodded, but from her expression, I knew she wasn't letting it go that easily. In fact,

I had a feeling she was about to blow it out of proportion.

"Young Sherlocks is on the case!" she announced, slapping the table.

Vanessa and I glanced at each other with zero surprise.

"Let's just go see what advice requests we have for the week, okay?" I grabbed Brooke's arm and picked up my lunch tray.

"Hey, have you thought any more about inviting you-know-who to the dance?" she asked.

I dropped my tray off at the garbage can. "So Tim and Greek yogurt, huh?"

Vanessa laughed. "Oooh. Shut down."

Brooke smirked and put her arm around me. "I think I figured out why you love popcorn so much."

I eyed her warily. "Why?"

"Well, popcorn comes from corn kernels, right? And you know who loves corn?"

"People who can't have gluten?"

"Chickens!" Brooke flapped her arms and made a clucking sound.

"Very nice," I said as we walked down the hall. "With your chicken noises and Tim's turkey calls, we could open a disappointing poultry farm."

"You are chicken, you know." Brooke poked me in the side. "You're afraid to ask him."

"What if I am?" I twisted out of her reach. "He's superpopular and I'm—"

"Superwonderful," said V, throwing her arms around me.

"Supersweet," added Brooke, hugging me from the other side.

"Thank you." I patted both their arms. "But just because you like me doesn't mean he does."

I fished a key from my pocket and unlocked the advice box.

"Want me to ask him for you?" Brooke leaned against the wall.

"That would be a huge <u>NO</u>, underlined and in all caps." I reached into the advice box and pulled out a handful of papers. "Here."

"Heather—"

"Let it go," Vanessa chided her. "It's like she said with Tim. If she wants our help, she'll ask."

I thumped the advice box. "And I know exactly where to go."

The three of us walked into the newsroom, said hello to Mrs. H, and settled in our section, sifting through advice requests that had come in since we'd turned in our material last Friday. Friday was our deadline, so issues could be back from the printers by Monday to distribute.

Gil walked by and tweaked Vanessa's shoulder, and she beamed at him. "Hey, you!"

"Hey yourself!" He shook his shaggy brown

hair out of his eyes, and his cheeks dimpled.

I watched their exchange with a smile, and Brooke leaned closer. "Don't you want that?"

I bopped her on the nose with my pen. "No talking about that. And no asking Tim about Greek yogurt," I added, spotting him out of the corner of my eye. He was chatting with Stefan, who looked tanner and taller than ever.

Stefan shook hair out of his eyes too, blond hair that looked soft and shiny without a hint of green, even though he spent a lot of time in the pool. He probably used a special shampoo. One that smelled like the ocean or stallions . . .

"Heather?" Brooke waved her hand in front of my face, and I sat up straight.

"Great advice!" I clapped my hands, hoping it was the right response.

Brooke had the latest issue spread on the desk in front of her. "Actually, I asked if you had some scissors."

I blushed and reached for my bag. "Yes, of course."

Tim joined us, and the rest of the class took their seats as Mrs. H called for attention.

"We're coming up on our Thanksgiving issue, which will run a week early since school's out for the holiday," she said. "But I thought it might be nice to have a few special features. We've got the front page doing one on the presidential pardon of turkeys, which many of you know was first done by Abraham Lincoln."

"Boo! Turkeys are delicious!" called Tim.

Several people laughed.

"And we also have our advice column working with Mary Patrick to put together a special feature with advice on how students can show their thanks during the holidays." She turned to Mary Patrick, who stepped forward.

"That's right. We'll be volunteering at a clothing collection center, the animal shelter, and a big brother and sister–type program called One Big Happy. Our first assignment is tomorrow at the clothing center," Mary Patrick continued. "Stefan, will you be able to take pictures?"

My heart beat a little faster, and I leaned forward in my seat.

"Sure," he said with a shrug.

Perfect! I settled back and smiled. A chance to be near Stefan without everyone else in school around. And since my friends wanted me to ask him out, I knew they wouldn't interfere.

Mrs. H ended her general announcements, and the class broke back into their sections.

"A clothing center!" V said with a squeal. "I'm so excited to see what they have."

"You know *we're* not getting the clothes," Brooke told her. "We're probably just sorting them by size."

"I know," she said. "But any day I get to put

my hands on fabric is a good day."

I smiled and picked up one of the advice requests, raising my eyebrows. "Wow. This one is for you." I passed it to Tim, who snickered and read it aloud.

"'Dear Lincoln's Letters, if I'm trying to impress a guy, should I act like one of the guys? I can already make fart noises with my armpit and am learning to burp the alphabet.'"

Brooke, Vanessa, and I laughed.

"And the answer is . . ." I gestured to Tim.

"Only act like a guy if you want to be seen as one of the guys." Tim folded up the note. "I'll put that one in the maybe pile." He fished around and read another one. "'Dear Lincoln's Letters, how do I get a guy to fall for me?'"

"Heather's," said Brooke and Vanessa at the same time.

I took the request slip, and as I read it, a tingle went up my spine.

Dear Lincoln's Letters,

I want to ask a guy to the Fall Into Winter dance, but how do I get him to fall for me first? I know we'll be perfect together, and he's really nice, but he never says more than hi.

Heartbroken in Homeroom

A girl in the exact same situation as me? This must be another sign. And if I answered her request, I could help her *and* myself without my friends finding out. I could even try the advice on Stefan and say it was for the column. Then I'd know for sure what he thought of me!

"I think I'll make this the one I answer this week," I said.

"But you haven't seen any of the others," said Brooke.

"I know, but it just feels right," I said, getting to my feet. "Do you think Mrs. H would let me go to the library?"

"What for?" asked Vanessa.

"So I can research the answer for my question and give this girl some options," I said. "You know our rules."

I was referring to the rule book we'd created for handling the advice column, the contents of which included a rule about researching what we didn't know and giving our readers different solutions, since one answer didn't necessarily fit all types of personalities.

"Sure," said Brooke.

Mrs. H was already talking to someone, so I strolled slowly toward her desk, lingering near Stefan's seat until he looked up.

"Hey, Heather," he said.

"Oh! Hey, Stefan!" I said in my best surprised voice. "What are you doing here?"

"I work on the newspaper. Same as you," he said with a crooked smile. "We're in this class together."

Dumb. Dumb. *Dumb*.

"Of course," I said with a laugh. "I meant what are you doing *now*? Not 'here.'"

"I'm trying to choose which photos to run for the piece on the turkey pardon. What do you think?"

I leaned closer to inspect the images just as Stefan brushed his hair back.

I wanted to say, *I think your hair smells like the ocean* and *stallions*, but all I did was point at the pictures and say, "That one."

"Yeah, I like it too," he agreed. "Good eye!"

"Thanks!" I blushed. My heart started beating faster.

I could do it. I could do it now. I could ask him to the Fall Into Winter dance.

"Hey, Mrs. H is free if you need to talk to her." Stefan pointed to the front of the room.

"Yep!" I said, and hurried away, completely abandoning my question by Stefan's desk.

I got the library pass from Mrs. H and returned to my desk to get my bag. "See you in history," I said to Brooke, and waved to Vanessa and Tim.

The library lights were dimmed for some seventh graders watching a presentation, but I already knew where I needed to look: the sports section.

Last month, "Lincoln's Letters" had answered a question on how to get a guy interested, and one of the ways we'd mentioned was to share the guy's interests. Since Stefan was big into swimming, it wouldn't hurt to have a few handy facts to throw out, even if it was just to keep me from talking about his shampoo.

I found a book on famous swimmers and took it to a table, pulling a pocket-size notepad from my bag. I glanced around to make sure nobody could see the pad, which had pages titled "Family," "Photography," and "Swimming."

Yes, my notepad was filled with Stefan-related topics.

Yes, I may have even named it "the S Files."

But here's why it wasn't creepy (or at least what I planned to tell my parents if it ever came up): Every new thing I learned about Stefan was a new way to connect with him. That wasn't creepy; that was romantic! Knowing someone so well that they didn't have to explain themselves . . . talk about a time-saver.

I flipped through the library book and wrote down a few of the swimmers' names, along with some fun facts. Then I looked at photos of what they wore, writing down some brand names. I'd read somewhere that guys like a girl with a sense of humor, and since we were going to a clothing collection center, I could make a joke about the lack of swimwear.

"Boy, swimmers sure don't want to part with their Speedos, am I right?" I'd say.

He'd laugh, I'd laugh, and then he'd say, "Is there something you've been wanting to ask me? Whatever it is, the answer is yes."

I sighed happily and returned the book to the shelf. Then I selected a few magazines from the rack that looked like they might have dating advice. I started with *Modern Girl*, which had an article on making a good impression and bullet points on the importance of a smile, making a guy laugh, and having something different to offer than all the other girls.

"Something different," I said to myself.

Just not, according to Tim, armpit farts and alphabet burps.

I thought for a moment and smiled. Stefan was going to see that I was as different as they came.

CHAPTER

3

"Penny Wishes"

"Can we stop by the music store?" I asked Bubbe when she picked me up from school that afternoon.

"The one close to the frozen yogurt place?" She pulled out of the school parking lot. "Sure, we can stop at both."

I shook my head. "The yogurt place is miles away."

"We have a car. I want yogurt. It's close," she said.

I laughed. "You and Mom use the same kind of logic."

"When I was a girl"—Bubbe wagged a finger at me—"the only way we got frozen yogurt was if we put regular yogurt outside and waited for winter. So what's at the music store?"

"Sheet music," I told her. "For a new song I want to suggest for choir."

"They take requests? Is it a choir or a piano lounge?" She laughed with her whole body. Thankfully, we were stopped at a red light.

I bit my lip. "Can you keep a secret?"

"Of course." She pretended to zip her lips.

"Remember how we were talking about signs?" I ran my fingers along the car door. "Well, the signs are telling me to ask a boy out."

She glanced my way and smiled. "Cupid's arrow finally struck? That's adorable."

"I want to learn the song because it's one of his favorites," I told her.

Bubbe clutched her hand to her chest. "Stop. You're killing me with cuteness!"

"You think it's an okay idea?" I asked.

She leaned over and kissed the top of my head. "I think this boy is a fool if he doesn't fall for you after hearing the voice of an angel."

Ten minutes later, Bubbe and I were in the music store, where she was plunking keys on a piano while I browsed the sheet music.

According to my research (aka eavesdropping on Stefan), his favorite band was Thunder Barrel, and luckily, there were several of their new songs in the rack. None of them screamed "Choir!," so I went with "Penny Wishes" because it had a nice message, a nice beat, and was the only song without any bad words.

I headed down the aisle toward my grandma. "Okay, I'm—"

The chimes at the shop door sounded, and in walked . . . Stefan.

Instantly, I dropped into a crouch.

Bubbe, who was still standing by the piano,

tilted her head and stared at me. "Are you okay?"

I nodded and put my fingers to my lips, pointing toward the door.

Ever so slowly, she swiveled her head, then looked back at me and nodded, strolling at her most casual pace toward me.

"That's the guy I'm trying to impress!" I whispered.

She paused beside me and browsed the sheet music. "Flirting has definitely changed since I was a girl."

"I want to surprise him with the song," I said. "So he can't know about it in advance. He doesn't even know I like him."

"Here." She reached down and handed me the sheet music for Aretha Franklin's "Respect."

"Very funny," I said.

"No, I wanted you to have something else to show him," she said. "Because he's coming this way."

"Ahh!" I glanced around for a place to hide, but in a music store, my options were to either twist my body into the shape of a guitar and hang from the wall or hide behind a massive speaker and lose my hearing. I tucked the "Penny Wishes" sheet music behind "Respect" and stood up just as Stefan rounded the corner into our aisle.

"Oh, hey, Heather!" he said. "What's going on?"

"Just buying some music for choir," I said, holding it up.

"Respect!" he said, beating his fist against his chest with a loud thump.

"What? Oh, right! Ha-ha!" I imitated him, wincing as my fist hit my own chest.

Luckily, Stefan didn't notice, instead holding a hand out to my grandma. "Hi, I go to school with your daughter."

"My daughter!" Bubbe whooped and elbowed me. "Such a charmer. Heather, you have"—I stared at her with wide eyes, and she cleared her throat—"a little something on your face."

Then she *licked her thumb* and rubbed it against my cheek.

My grandma was grooming me in public.

"Thank you." I pulled her hand down and smiled at Stefan. "My grandma and I should be going. See you tomorrow!" I took Bubbe's hand and pulled her toward the exit.

"Heather, wait!" Stefan called after me, and my heart skipped several beats. In fact, I'm pretty sure it changed to a totally different rhythm.

I put on my best smile and turned. "Yes?"

"I think you have to pay for that first." He pointed to the sheet music in my hand.

"Oh." I looked down at it. "Right."

I pivoted on my heel and pulled Bubbe toward the checkout counter.

When we got back to the car, she gave me an apologetic smile. "Sorry, honey. I guess I'm no better around boys."

"It's okay," I said with a smile. "You're family. You're supposed to embarrass me."

"*And*"—she put the car in gear—"take you out for frozen yogurt."

The next morning I arrived at school extra early to show the choral director Miss Thompson the Thunder Barrel sheet music.

"What's this?" she asked when I handed it to her. Then her eyes lit up. "Is it your song for solo tryouts? Heather, I can't tell you how happy—"

"No, no, no." I shook my head until my hair fanned out around me. "I'm not trying out."

Miss Thompson lowered the music and sighed. "Heather, I really think you should."

"It's too much pressure and attention. I like being part of the choir, not apart from it."

Miss Thompson gave a defeated shrug. "All right, then. What is this music for?"

"Just a little something different. Could we

try it out?" I asked. "It would be nice to have a couple songs that the students could relate to."

Miss Thompson scanned the sheet music, bopping her head side to side as if imagining the tune. After a moment she said, "I don't see why we can't try it out just for fun."

She put the first page of the music on the overhead projector, and as students trickled into the choir room, they glanced up and whispered excitedly.

"Sweet! Are we really doing this?" asked Emmett Elders.

"I'm humoring Heather," Miss Thompson said with a smile.

"Nice!" He held a hand up to me, and I high-fived it.

Emmett was a sixth grader who'd transferred in from private school but still treated everyone like we'd all gone to school together forever. Even though he had the pink cheeks and curly blond hair of a cherub, his voice was the deepest of anyone in our grade. The first time anyone ever hears him, they blink and stare.

He settled in with the few other guys who formed the bass, and I joined the altos.

Even though I'd suggested "Penny Wishes" for purely selfish reasons, it made me feel good to know that everyone enjoyed it so much. I focused on getting the melody just right and followed the tempo closely.

Since I'd added another song to our rotation, practice ran all the way up until the bell for homeroom, so I didn't get a chance to catch up with Brooke, V, and Tim, but the rest of the morning, I hummed "Penny Wishes" under my breath. In my advanced math class, when we were supposed to be solving for X, Emmett, who sat next to me, hummed along when he heard me. We both continued to look at our papers, but out of the corner of my eye, I saw him smile, and I smiled back.

Stefan was definitely going to be blown away that afternoon.

At lunchtime, Brooke was in full planning mode for our trip to the clothing drop-off center.

"So I checked with Mary Patrick, and it's just like I thought. We'll be sorting clothing donations and throwing out the stuff that's ripped or damaged or stained. . . ." She made a face. "We may want to bring gloves."

"What time are we getting there?" asked Tim. "I have hockey practice at six o'clock."

"We're going right after school," said Brooke. "So you should have plenty of time."

"And Stefan's going to be there to take pictures?" I asked as casually as possible.

But not casually enough.

Vanessa and Brooke exchanged a look and smiled.

"You know," said Tim, "I have enough trouble handling Stefan doing school hours. I'd rather not be around him any more than I have to. Can we have Gil take pictures instead?"

"No!" I squealed, and Tim jumped. "I mean, he's probably busy working on the horoscope. Studying the stars and . . ." I shrugged.

"The stars don't come out until after dark," said Tim. "And I'm pretty sure he just makes the horoscopes up."

"He does not!" cried Vanessa.

"Do you know how he gets them?" asked Brooke.

"I do not!" she cried, and we all laughed. "I've honestly never thought to ask."

"Either way, he's probably busy," I said. "Stefan is the best guy for the job."

"Oh, I get it." Tim rolled his eyes. "You still have a crush. What do you think's so great about him?"

"Everything!" I gushed. "His hair, his smile, his eyes . . ."

"Every single person at this school has hair, a smile, and eyes," said Tim. "My *point*, Heather, is that all the things you like about Stefan are superficial."

I frowned. "That's not true! I think he's an excellent swimmer and a brilliant photographer, and he was really sweet to me after the advice-off when I had to stand in for Vanessa."

Poor V had gotten stage fright and asked me to speak in her place, which I'd botched horribly. To cheer me up afterward, Stefan had taken me with him to photograph butterflies at an exhibit that was visiting the school. It was magical to watch the butterflies flutter all around us and land softly on our shoulders and arms.

"Look, I'm not saying the guy doesn't have his moments," said Tim. "But he's not boyfriend material."

"Oh, and you are?" I shot back.

The table got quiet.

Vanessa became incredibly interested in her sandwich, and Brooke looked between me and Tim.

"Sorry," I said, shaking my head. "That was mean of me to say. I just felt like I was under attack."

Tim's expression was solemn, but he nodded. "You're right. *I'm* sorry."

There was silence for a moment, and then Brooke sighed.

"Dullest. Fight. Ever."

"What did you expect?" I asked, glad to move away from the awkwardness. "There aren't any folding chairs for me to hit him with."

"Yeah, and I already drank my soda, so throwing it in Heather's face is out," said Tim.

V snorted. "I love how Heather fights like a wrestler and Tim fights like a soap-opera villain."

"Hey, soda throwing can be pretty hardcore," said Tim. He lifted his cup and made a muscle. "Especially if it's boiling-hot soda."

"Ew." Brooke wrinkled her nose. "Hot soda is the worst."

Our conversation shifted to the worst things we'd ever eaten or drank, but the whole time, in the back of my mind, I replayed Tim's words to me. And the fact that neither of my friends had argued with him.

When the bell rang to end lunch, all four of us headed for the newsroom, Vanessa arguing with Brooke over whether rotten tomatoes or rotten apples were worse.

"It wasn't a rotten tomato that put Snow White in a coma," pointed out Brooke when we stopped to check the advice box.

"And it wasn't a rotten apple either," said Vanessa.

"And she wasn't in a coma," said Tim. "She

was in a parallel universe."

Brooke froze with her hand in the advice box and turned to stare at him. Vanessa and I were already one step ahead of her, gaping at Tim, wide-eyed.

He looked from me to Brooke to Vanessa before throwing his arms in the air. "Okay, I saw *Stealing Ever After* last night! Gabby dragged me to it."

Gabby was Tim's twin sister.

"She dragged you to it. Right," said Brooke. "You didn't have any desire to see it yourself."

Tim shot her a withering look. "If I really wanted to see a romantic fairy-tale movie, you think I would've taken my *sister*?"

"So what did you think of it?" I asked.

He studied the floor. "It was action-packed and a thrill-a-minute."

Brooke, Vanessa, and I cheered.

"What was your favorite part?" I asked.

"Did you cry at the end?" Brooke asked.

"Who had the best dress?" Vanessa asked.

"Hey, look! Advice requests!" said Tim, taking them out of Brooke's hand and heading into the newsroom.

Brooke shrugged at me and V. "I guess that's all we're getting out of him." Her eyes brightened. "Hey! Do you think that's why he was acting suspicious yesterday?"

"Yes," I said, even though I didn't. I was just hoping she'd drop it and leave poor Tim alone.

We walked into the newsroom and saw Mary Patrick crouched beside Tim in earnest conversation. As soon as they saw us, they both straightened up.

"So I'll be expecting that article tomorrow," Mary Patrick told him.

"What article?" asked Brooke, dropping into her seat.

"Something for the sports section," said Tim.

"Now, about this afternoon," Mary Patrick said, looking at all four of us. "Do you have rides to the collection center? If not, Mrs. H still has room in her car."

That had been an unfortunate twist, having a teacher along to watch us. But hopefully, she'd be too busy talking to the staff to pay attention.

"My mom is going to take us," said Vanessa, "and then Brooke's dad is going to pick us up on his way home from work."

Mary Patrick nodded. "Then Mrs. H, Stefan, and I will meet you guys in the lobby of the building. We're only staying for a little while," she said. "He's going to take a few photos, and I'm going to make sure you guys know what you're doing."

"Sorting clothes *can* be a real head-scratcher," said Brooke.

Mary Patrick ignored her. "When you guys

are doing the charity assignments, I want you to think of the pros and cons for each one." She paused. "I'll be writing the informative part of the article, but I want you to choose one person to write about how the experiences made you feel. Whoever's the best at tugging heartstrings."

Tim chuckled. "Well, I wouldn't say I'm the best—"

"Not you, dork," said Brooke. "We want people helping out because it's the right thing to do, not because they like you."

"Can't it be both?" he asked.

Vanessa pointed at me. "I think it should be Heather."

I smiled and sat up a little taller. "Me too!"

"Me three," said Brooke.

"I think that's the best choice too," said Mary Patrick. "Sorry, Tim."

He shrugged. "I can't argue with that choice."

Mrs. H clapped her hands at the front of the classroom, and Mary Patrick hurried away to join her for announcements.

"How did your research go yesterday?" Brooke asked me.

"Pretty good," I said. "I think I'll really be able to help this reader out." *And myself,* I thought.

"Oh! Speaking of which, I almost forgot that I brought you something." Vanessa reached into her book bag and pulled out a few teen magazines and some purple sheets of paper. "I was looking at them for the clothes, but I saw they also had some helpful dating tips."

"Perfect! Thanks!"

"And I wanted both of you to be the first to hear about something special Katie and I are doing." She handed Brooke and me the purple sheets.

"How come I don't get one?" asked Tim.

"I'm pretty sure you wouldn't be interested," said V.

Brooke and I looked at our papers and laughed when we realized what she meant.

Need help with your makeup or dress
for the Fall Into Winter dance?
Call KV Fashions. We'll turn you from
drab to fab!

"Here you go, buddy," said Brooke, handing it to him.

Tim scanned the page and smiled. "You're right. I've got it all locked up."

"This is a great idea!" I told V, waving the flyer.

"Thanks! I was hoping to put an ad in the newspaper, but Mrs. H won't let us because then it would seem like the school was favoring our business."

"Try Locker 411," said Brooke.

Vanessa smacked herself on the forehead. "Duh!"

Locker 411 was an invention of Gabby's, the former owner of locker number 411. It was packed with binders full of information to help the girls at our school cope with the perils of everyday life. It was an instant hit, and girls have been adding their own tidbits ever since. Last month, we even advertised the advice-off there.

"Thanks, Brooke. That's brilliant," said Vanessa. Then almost shyly, she added, "Are you going to let us do your makeup for the dance? We'll give you a good deal."

"Sure," she said with a shrug. "It might be nice for Abel to see me in something other than cherry lip balm."

"Great!" Vanessa turned to me. "I know you

haven't asked anyone yet, but when you do . . ."

"I'd love to have your help," I told her with a nod of my head. "When I get a date."

Which, I thought, *could be this very afternoon.*

4

Clothes Encounter

"Everyone take a pair," Vanessa said from the front seat of her mom's car. She reached back, holding a pile of latex gloves in one hand.

"Do I want to ask where you got these?" asked Brooke, reaching for them with just the tips of her fingers.

"The nurse's office," said V.

Our responses from the backseat were less than thrilled.

"Gross!"

"Ew!"

"You've taken recycling too far!"

"Oh, for the love of—" Vanessa divided the gloves into three pairs and threw them at each of us. "They're not used, dingbats. Nurse Patti got them for me fresh out of a new box."

"For being such a loyal customer?" asked Tim, shaking out his gloves.

Since Vanessa's so accident-prone, she tends to visit the nurse more than the average person.

Her mom pulled up in front of the clothing donation center, and Vanessa opened her car door with a flourish, as if she was red carpet–bound.

I'm not sure what I expected, but when we walked through the front door, it was just like being in a department store. Music played from overhead speakers, and there were racks of clothing, dressing rooms to one side, and a checkout area on the other. I removed my gloves as subtly as possible, and my friends did the same.

"Where are the others?" I asked, though I

secretly meant, "Where's Stefan?"

I spotted him in the men's section, a tank top draped against the front of his shirt.

"Ten bucks says he'd wear it like that if his mom didn't dress him," said Tim. I elbowed him.

"Stefan doesn't live with his mom. He lives with his dad and stepmom."

Tim whistled. "Wow, you can learn a lot about someone by watching them from the bushes."

Before I could retort, Mary Patrick's voice boomed across the room.

"Advice team!" She was standing near the checkout counter, talking with a woman who had short spiky hair and wore a painter's smock. When we all glanced over, she beckoned us.

"You know we have names," said Brooke as we approached.

"Yes, but if I name you, then it makes it even harder to get rid of you," Mary Patrick said. She gestured to the woman beside her. "This is

Sally Finch, by the way."

"You can call me Sal." The woman extended her hand, and we took turns shaking it. "Thanks for volunteering your time. I think when you see what we do, you'll appreciate your old clothes even more." She held up a finger. "But hopefully not so much that you won't donate them to us."

We smiled.

"Why don't you come with me to the back?" Sal pushed through a door behind the cash registers, and we followed.

She gave us a quick tour while Stefan snapped pictures.

"We start with the collection corner," she said, pointing out a pile of bags and other containers, "which can hold anything from clothes to shoes to hats. Accessories go in one container to be inspected and shelved, and clothes go in these." She patted wheeled laundry bins and pushed one toward some giant steel machines with round windows on the front.

"We have industrial-sized washing machines and dryers to clean the donations that come through." Sal spoke loudly above the rumble and gush of water in one of the machines.

"What about ripped clothes?" asked Brooke.

Sal shook her head. "Unfortunately, we don't have the manpower to mend things, so we either sell them on a clearance rack or use them for rags."

"How many donations do you get a day?" asked Tim.

"Not as many for kids as we'd like," she said. "I guess parents either use them as hand-me-downs or they're in such bad shape, they don't bother to donate. Plus, we sell them for so much cheaper than adult clothes that they get scooped up pretty quick."

"I'm surprised you don't just give all the

clothes away," I said. "I mean, they're already used."

"You think they could stay in business if they didn't make any money?" asked Tim with a snort.

"Actually, we're strictly nonprofit," said Sal. "A local church bought us the building space, so only a small portion of the money we take in goes toward keeping the lights on. Most of the money goes toward people who need a little help getting back on their feet."

"That's amazing," I said. "All from clothes?"

Sal nodded. "And so many people just throw things away when they get too small. Imagine if everyone donated."

"So where do we get started?" asked Brooke, rubbing her hands together.

Sal led us to a table with clothing strewn across it. "These are the latest cleaned donations. Look at the size and style, and if they're in good shape, put them in men's, women's, or children's bins." She pointed to three more rolling laundry baskets with labels on them.

"While they work, we'd love to speak with you a little more in-depth," said Mary Patrick, pointing to herself and Mrs. H.

"And I'd love to take a few more pictures," said Stefan.

"Of course," Sal said with a nod.

"Okay!" Brooke clapped her hands at the rest of us. "Let's spread out and start sorting." She leaned closer. "And if you want to make a game out of it, we can shoot baskets into the bins." She grabbed a pair of jeans and tossed them into a bin.

"You didn't even look at them!" I said, pulling the jeans back out and inspecting them.

"They're jeans." Brooke shrugged. "Jeans are indestructible."

"Ugh. Tights are not." Vanessa lifted a pair up

by a leg and dropped them onto the floor. "Who donates tights, anyway? That's like donating underwear."

Tim grabbed a shirt and examined it. "Good." He spun and tossed the shirt into the men's bin.

I picked up a T-shirt that had a hole in the armpit. "Not good." I dropped it on the floor, where I saw a small pile already growing at Vanessa's feet. "V?"

"Ugh. No. No. Tragic." Vanessa picked up various shirts and dropped them on the floor.

"What are you doing?" I asked, picking one up. "This one's okay."

Vanessa stared at me in horror. "It's mustard colored! It'll never be okay."

I rolled my eyes. "I think some people care more about staying warm than being fashionable." I put the shirt in the bin of women's things and bent to pick up something else she'd tossed. "This is fine too."

"Sal told us to look at the style, and that collar isn't in style anymore," she said.

"I think she meant style as in gender," said Tim.

"I choose to interpret it differently," said V with a shrug.

"We're here to help these people," said Brooke. She balled up a sock and threw it at V, who caught it in midair.

"I *am* helping," she said. "Just because someone's on a budget doesn't mean they can't still look good." She threw a puffy coat on top of the other discards.

At that moment, Sal walked by and paused at the pile of clothes by Vanessa's feet. "What's all this?"

"Fashion rejects." Vanessa made a thumbs-down motion. "Trust me. I'm doing everyone a favor."

Sal crooked a finger at her. "Come with me.

All of you. I want you to see something."

The four of us, Stefan, Mary Patrick, and Mrs. H walked with her into the main part of the store. Sal stopped just behind the registers, and we all gathered around.

"Mrs. Delaney is one of our regulars," she said in a low voice, pointing under the counter in the direction of the kids' clothing. A woman with a baby strapped to her front was pushing a stroller with one hand and holding a little girl's hand in the other. "She has to make ends meet on her own."

Stefan raised his camera to take a picture, but Tim pushed it down. "Not of them, dude."

We watched as Mrs. Delaney searched the few racks of kids' clothing and pulled out a child-sized puffy coat similar to the one Vanessa had put in the discard pile. Mrs. Delaney held it up and turned it on the hanger before checking the price tag. She smiled and offered it to her daughter. With a happy squeal, the little girl beamed and hugged the coat to her, wiggling from side to side.

My heart almost burst at the cuteness.

"See, it might not be totally in style and it might not be new, but it's hers," said Sal in a quiet voice.

V nodded but didn't say anything, her eyes filling with tears. I stepped closer and put my arm around her.

"Every donation is a gift," continued Sal. "Not garbage."

"I'm . . . I'm sorry," said Vanessa, wringing her hands together.

Sal smiled and squeezed her shoulder. "Your heart's in the right place. But here, fashion isn't as important as staying warm."

Vanessa wiped her eyes and looked up at Sal. "I have tons of old clothes I could bring! I don't wear half of them anymore!"

"I'm sure everyone on the newspaper has something they could donate," spoke up Mrs. H. "We can bring it up in class tomorrow."

"Anything would be appreciated," said Sal with a grateful smile.

"Come on, V," Brooke said, bumping her arm. "Let's get some more clothes on those racks."

Vanessa wiped her eyes and nodded, pushing through the door to the sorting room. She scooped up all the clothes she'd dropped and started putting them in bins. Occasionally, she gave a certain item a disgusted look, but nothing else touched the floor.

Soon, my friends and I were working side by side in silence while Mary Patrick and Mrs. H talked to Sal, and Stefan's camera clicked behind us. I watched him walk the room, taking pictures from different angles. After a few more minutes, he checked his phone.

"My dad should be here in a minute to pick

me up. Mary Patrick, are you hitching a ride?"

He was leaving! And I hadn't shown him how awesome I was yet!

"Heather, you okay?" asked Brooke. "You've got that turtleneck in a chokehold."

It was now or never. I took a deep breath, placed the turtleneck in one of the bins, and started to sing, just like I did when I folded laundry at home.

Penny throws a copper coin into the well.
She doesn't know what else to try.

Tim kept working, but Brooke and Vanessa stopped and smiled at each other. Unless they sign me up for karaoke songs, I never sing on my own in public.

Stefan smiled as he reviewed his pictures. I raised my voice a little.

Can her luck be changed, can wishing break
the spell
Or ever will she cry?

Now, Stefan was humming under his breath.
I kept going, pulling another shirt from the pile.

The nights grow cold, the nights grow long.
It's hard to tell the right from wrong.
Each coin she steals goes toward a meal
Except for all the . . . Penny wishes.

"I love that song!" said Stefan. "I didn't think
it was your type of music."

"Oh, yeah! I like all kinds of . . . that music," I
explained.

He raised the camera and took my picture.
"Keep going!"

I opened my mouth to start the next verse, but

someone else got to it before I could. I glanced at my friends, who weren't singing but were looking at a woman with her hair in a bandana, crooning the lyrics to "Penny Wishes" in a smoky, deep voice.

"'Many years go by, and there's much more to tell,'" she sang. "'Her wishes start to change.'"

Stefan turned his camera in her direction.

No way was this happening.

I started singing even louder than the woman in the bandana. "'She met a sweet young lad, and deep in love she fell.'"

She looked surprised (okay, everyone did) but increased the volume of *her* voice. Stefan watched both of us with a huge smile but couldn't set his attention in one place.

I felt around for Brooke's foot and stepped on it.

"Owww . . . 'the nights grow cold,'" Brooke belted out the chorus, which wasn't remotely close to where we were in the song. But it seemed to throw the woman in the bandana off, so I joined in. Vanessa chimed in too, throwing in a few dramatic arm gestures, the last of which was smacking Tim in the back of the head. He rolled his eyes and started singing too. Stefan held his camera at arm's length and took a picture of all of us singing, his head so close to mine I could feel his bangs tickle my face.

Mrs. H smiled at our performance, and Mary Patrick just watched with her arms crossed.

When we got to the final line, "'All because of . . . Penny wishes!,'" Sal applauded.

"I've heard of whistling while you work, but that was much better," she said with a laugh.

"That was awesome," agreed Stefan.

"I hate to spoil the encore, but we have to go," Mary Patrick told him, pointing to her watch. "Are you four okay to work alone?"

"Of course!" said Brooke. "We've got it under control."

Mary Patrick shook hands with Sal and headed for the front of the store.

"Any time you want to have another impromptu singalong, you let me know." Stefan winked at me and waved to everyone else before chasing after Mary Patrick.

My friends all turned to look at me, and I shrugged. "It's a really good song."

But in my head there was a standing ovation and roses being thrown at my feet, with Stefan handing me an entire bouquet.

When I got home that night, the first thing I did was sit on the couch next to Bubbe and hug her.

"Oh, I'm guessing it was a good day," she said with a smile, patting my arm.

I told her what had happened, and she squeezed me tight, kissing my cheek.

"I'm so proud of you for going after what you want!" she said. "What's next?"

"What's next?" I repeated with a frown.

"You've baited the hook," she said. "How are you going to reel him in?"

"I . . . will have to get back with you on that," I said, getting to my feet. "After a little more research."

I shouted hello to my parents and Isaac and promised to fill them in on volunteering at the clothing donation center. Then I hurried up to my room, pulling out all the magazines V had given me. I had to act while Stefan was still thinking of me and that song.

A couple of the magazines were a bust, only talking about sweet dates for couples and quick ways to patch up a fight. "Still a little early for that," I mumbled to myself. The third magazine literally had an article with the title "Ways to Reel Him In."

"Bingo!" I flipped to the piece and started reading. Some of the tips were things I'd never do, like "crack him up every chance you get!" I wasn't a comedian. But I could, as the article suggested, make sure I stayed on his mind.

I searched on the internet for a few more bands that were like Thunder Barrel and wrote down the names. My plan was to suggest them to Stefan the next morning.

I practiced in the bathroom mirror. "Hey! I know you like Thunder Barrel, but here are some other bands you might really enjoy!"

I made a face at my reflection. "You sound like a TV commercial."

"What are you doing?" Isaac asked from the doorway.

"Oh, hey!" I whirled around, knocking the soap dispenser into the sink and sending a hairbrush flying.

He smirked. "What did I catch you at?"

"Nothing! You just startled me." I moved around, setting everything right. "I was practicing something for school."

"Sure," he said. "Well, when you get done 'practicing for school'"—he made air quotes—"come downstairs for dinner."

I made a face but followed him into the dining room, where my mom was marveling over a brisket my dad had made. Then, as I told them about my day, she marveled over me.

"I love how you kids are doing such good work," she said, pointing her fork at me. Then she nodded to my brother. "You should take a page from her book."

Isaac snorted. "Your daughter talks to herself in the bathroom mirror like the wicked queen from that dopey movie."

"It's not dopey, it's good!" I said. "Me and my friends are even going to see—" I froze and a smile crept over my face. "Oh, you are brilliant!"

I leaped up and ran around the table to hug my brother.

"Ahh! Your fork is in my shoulder!" he yelped.

But I didn't care. My brother had given me the perfect way to reel in Stefan.

It was time for the newspaper staff to go on a little group date.

CHAPTER 5

Stefan's Great Idea

The next morning, I put on my cutest green top (Stefan's favorite color) and braided my hair in pigtails (which Stefan had told me looked cute on October 14). I even dabbed on a little lip gloss, which I normally hate because it draws attention to the gap in my front teeth.

When Bubbe walked out of the kitchen with her travel mug of coffee, she raised an eyebrow. "My, my. Aren't we adorable?"

I did a half curtsy. "I heard once that if you want to feel confident, you should wear something that makes you feel good about yourself."

I'd actually read it in one of Vanessa's magazines just the night before, but it seemed to be working. I felt pretty confident as we strolled out the front door and got in the car.

"So what's the plan?" she asked, buckling in.

"A group date," I said. "That way there's less pressure on him, and he can see me at my very best when I'm with my friends."

"I like it!" said Bubbe, toasting me with her mug of coffee.

Since I wasn't in a hurry to get to school this time, there were already several kids in the choir room when I showed up.

And there was another new song on the overhead.

I couldn't help smiling to myself. I'd set a trend. I never set trends. If anything, I was the one who killed them by finally giving in and following them. Vanessa was going to have to hear about this.

I didn't recognize the title of the song, but I recognized the name of the band as one I'd written down to mention to Stefan.

Emmett walked up beside me and nudged me. "Hey, you like my pick?"

"This is yours?" I asked.

He shrugged as if it was no big deal, but the smile on his face said otherwise. "I figured I'd give it a shot as long as Miss Thompson was in the mood to let us try new things. If you liked Thunder Barrel, you'll definitely like this band."

I nodded. It was perfect, actually. If I was going to recommend other bands to Stefan, I should at least know their music.

Emmett crossed his arms and stared up at the projection. "So did you ask anyone special to Fall Into Winter yet?"

I turned to stare at him. Unbelievable. Not only was Brooke bugging me to ask Stefan, but now she was getting other people involved?

Emmett saw the look on my face and shoved his hands into his pockets. "What?"

I tapped my chin. "I'm guessing someone put you up to this."

Emmett blushed and studied the floor. "How did you know?"

"Wow." I shook my head. "I wonder if she's going to have the lunch lady send me messages in my alphabet soup!" I walked off to text Brooke.

You're sweet to worry about my dating life, but please don't. I've got a plan! ☺

"Cell phones away!" called Miss Thompson as she approached her lectern. "Let's get this practice started."

All of us knew how to read music, but the tempo still felt off, even with Miss Thompson counting the beat. Plus, "Penny Wishes" was a sweet song about hoping for more, while Emmett's choice was about a girl who ended up going blind.

"That was an . . . interesting choice," said Miss Thompson when we'd finished. In a quieter voice she added, "I probably should have read all the way to the end of the song."

"Sorry," said Emmett, digging his hands into his pockets again.

"It's fine," said Miss Thompson with a dismissive wave. "Although maybe we'll stick with more traditional songs."

And just like that, the trend I'd started died after a day.

That seemed about right.

At the end of practice, I walked up to Emmett, who was being teased by his friends.

"Hey, it was a good try," I told him with an encouraging smile. "If we were a goth metal choir, it would've been perfect."

He and his friends laughed. "Well, we have black robes, so we're off to a good start," he said.

I waved good-bye and then hurried to my

homeroom, but someone called after me.

"Hey, Heather, wait up!"

I turned and saw Jeffrey Lee sprinting toward me. He was one of the few eighth graders I knew outside Journalism, since we had choir and Model United Nations together.

"Two things," he said, catching his breath. "We have a MUN emergency meeting tomorrow before school."

Jeffrey was also the secretary-general in charge of Model UN.

"Emergency?" I asked. "Is everything okay?"

He nodded. "Great Britain and Canada were dating, but they got in a fight about who's more important, and now they don't want to be in the same room together."

"But the whole debate this year is about Great Britain," I said. "And the whole point of MUN is peaceful resolution."

"Ironic, right?" he said with a smirk. "Anyway,

I just cleared it with Miss Thompson, so can you skip choir tomorrow and join us?"

I nodded. "Of course. What was the other thing you wanted to ask?"

He sighed. "I know it's none of my business, but the Fall Into Winter dance is next weekend, and a friend of mine is hoping you'll ask him."

My heart skipped a beat. "Who?"

Jeffrey smiled. "He'd rather I not say. Do you have any plans for the dance?"

"I have someone in mind," I said cagily. "He'll know after this weekend."

"Great! I'll pass that along." The first warning bell sounded, and he made a face. "I've gotta go. See you tomorrow morning!"

"Bye!" I said, turning toward my homeroom.

Katie was standing outside the door of hers. "Somebody has a crush on you!" she sang.

"Maybe," I said with a smile. "But who?"

"Isn't it obvs? That guy's in the eighth grade,

right?" She pointed to where Jeffrey had been, and I nodded. "It's gotta be one of his classmates."

"You think?" I said in a voice that came out squeaky. I'd secretly been hoping the same thing. I mean, Stefan was an eighth grader, but what else did they have in common? Stefan liked to swim, he was a photographer, he was a sportswriter. . . .

I suddenly grabbed Katie's hands, jumping up and down. "Jeffrey's on the basketball team!"

She jumped up and down with me. "I don't know what that means!"

The second bell rang, and I released her hands.

"Talk to you later!" I said.

"Wait, wait! Take one of these." She handed me a purple flyer.

"I already have one," I said.

"Not the new version," she said. "We just printed them last night! With one little change."

She pointed to the payment line, and I smiled. It said:

Please bring one fabulous piece of used
clothing.

"Here." I hugged Katie. "Give that to Vanessa if you see her before I do."

"Okay," said Katie with a laugh. "And make sure you ask your Prince Charming to the ball!"

I would. But first I had to make sure the opportunity presented itself.

Since I was in honors classes, I didn't see my friends until lunchtime to share my idea.

Vanessa was the first one there, eating a tuna sandwich.

"Hey, you!" I waved to her. "Did Katie give you that hug from me?"

Vanessa swallowed and then smiled. "Yes, but I already spent it on Gil."

"That," I said, "is adorable. And I love your new fee for a makeover."

V shrugged. "It's the least we can do, you know?"

"What are we talking about?" asked Brooke, throwing down her lunch bag.

"Katie and Vanessa's good deed," I said. I handed her the flyer, but she waved it away.

"Awesome, but I saw it in homeroom. Where's Tim? I want to talk to everyone about tomorrow afternoon."

We'd be visiting the animal shelter, and I, for one, couldn't wait. Isaac was allergic to animal dander, so we'd never be getting a fur baby at our house unless we shaved it first.

"I'm not sure," I said. "But before he gets here, can I talk to you guys about something?"

I had no desire to fight with Tim over a group date with Stefan.

"Sure," said Vanessa. "Is everything okay?"

"It is," I said. "And I was wondering what you guys thought of a group . . . outing for the whole news team. You know . . . as a team-builder."

"And what a happy coincidence that Stefan is on that team!" said Brooke, feigning surprise.

I sighed. Apparently, I was more transparent than I thought. "Fine, yes."

Brooke pounded her fist on the table. "I like it! You're taking action."

Vanessa waved a hand. "One problem, though. If a sixth grader suggests this, nobody is going to want to go." She gave me an apologetic smile. "No offense, sweetie."

"No, you're right," I said. "Someone else will have to bring it up."

Brooke snapped her fingers. "Get Stefan to do it! You know he's going to love being the one who gets the credit, and because he came up with it, he'll have to be there."

"Brilliant!" I said. "Thanks!" At that moment,

I spotted Tim. "And just keep this between us, okay?"

"Of course," said Vanessa.

"Here's something I've always wanted to know." Tim put his lunch tray down next to mine. "Why do girls always gather in groups and whisper?"

"We're plotting to take over the world," said Brooke.

Tim smirked and opened his soda. "Is there a different evil plan per group, or is it the same one for all of you?"

"Same plan," I said. "But it's less likely you'll hear us in smaller groups."

"But every year we hold a meeting for all females around the planet," said Vanessa. "We call it Fashion Week."

Brooke elbowed her. "We've already said too much."

After lunch, while Brooke and Vanessa

distracted Tim at the advice request box, I approached Stefan on my own.

"Hey, Stefan? Do you have a second?"

"Sure! Loving the green shirt, by the way."

Score one for the S Files.

"Thanks. I'm trying to put together a team-builder for Journalism, and I could really use your help," I told him.

"My help?" He sat a little taller. "Of course. What's up?"

"I want to get everyone to go to the movies on Saturday to see *Stealing Ever After*." I cleared my throat and played dumb. "Have you seen it?"

He nodded. "Great movie."

I leaned in confidentially. "Well, I'm having trouble convincing everyone to go." My friends walked in at that moment, and I jerked my head in Tim's direction, rolling my eyes. "I think if you suggested it, everyone would want to come."

Stefan smiled. "You have a point."

I took a deep breath. "Would you be free on Saturday to go?"

He thought for a moment. "Not at night, but a matinee, sure."

"Good enough," I said with a smile. "Will you help me out?" I clasped my hands in front of my chest and considered batting my eyelashes, but decided it might be a step too far.

He puffed up his chest and got to his feet. "Hey, guys? Guys!" he shouted to the rest of the class. Everyone turned to look at him. "I think this news team could really use a boost of morals."

I winced but didn't correct him.

"Why don't we all go to the movies this weekend as a team and see . . ." He paused dramatically, "*Stealing Ever After.*"

The girls in the class squealed and chattered excitedly, but the guys groaned and grumbled.

"I think that's a wonderful idea!" Mrs. H

clasped her hands together.

We settled on the time and meet-up location, and Mrs. H announced that it was time to start class. She called on each section for updates, and when it came to the advice column, Brooke told the class about our trip to the donation center.

"They really need lots of kids' clothes, guys," she finished.

"That being said," interjected Mary Patrick, "we've set up a collection box by the advice column request box outside the classroom. Just make sure your donations are in good shape."

We broke into our small groups, and Brooke said, "Don't forget tomorrow is our day at the animal shelter, so bring a change of clothes that you don't mind getting . . . um . . . pooped on."

"Or punctured with teeth marks and claw marks," added Tim. "But if any of the above happens, please have Stefan take a picture of it."

Brooke, Vanessa, and I exchanged looks.

"You're not going?" asked Brooke.

He shook his head. "I have a thing."

"'A thing'?" repeated Brooke. "Could you be more specific?"

"I could," he said. "But I choose not to."

"Does it have to do with Greek yogurt?" asked Vanessa.

Tim reached into the pile of advice slips. "Sure, why not."

"Okay, well, we can see about rescheduling the shelter to next week," said Brooke.

Tim shook his head. "I'll be busy next week, too." Before Brooke could interject, he added, "I already cleared this with Mary Patrick."

"So she knows your big secret, but you won't tell us?" asked Vanessa.

For once, I had to agree. It was starting to seem fishy.

"Tim, are you in some sort of trouble?" I asked.

"Are those guys in the locker room messing

with you again?" Brooke narrowed her eyes.

Since Tim's position at the paper had made him popular with the girls, he'd picked up more than his fair share of enemies.

"No, it's nothing like that," he said.

"If we guess it right, will you tell us?" asked Brooke.

Tim chuckled. "Oh, you'll never guess."

"Well, promise if you need our help with anything, you won't be too afraid to ask," I said. "We may be plotting to take over the world, but we can help you in the meantime."

Vanessa and Brooke laughed.

"Thank you," said Tim. "And this one is for you."

He slid an advice request over to me. It was a girl asking how to handle a tagalong friend.

I jotted a quick line in my notebook: *Ask whoever you want to come in private and make it clear it's an exclusive invitation.*

Across from me, Brooke started giggling.

"What'd you get?" asked Vanessa, reading over her shoulder. Then she started giggling too.

Tim looked at me. "I feel like this might be a setup."

Brooke shook her head and read, "'Dear Lincoln's Letters, will you please tell my brother that the lime Jell-O in the cafeteria is safe to eat? He keeps thinking he'll turn into the Incredible Hulk.'"

Tim smiled. "Okay, that's pretty good."

"Ooh! Here's a perfect one," said V. "It's a girl wanting makeup tips for the Fall Into Winter dance. And I know just where to send her." V picked up her pen, but Brooke put a hand over it.

"If you're going to suggest your little side business, you can forget it."

"We can't use the column for personal gain," Tim reminded her. "Rule number 9."

"Aww, man!" She made a face and shrugged.

"Well, I'm still going to help her."

We worked through some more advice requests, and at the end of class, Brooke grabbed my hand and whispered, "Come on. I know exactly where we can get the answers about Tim."

She rushed me to our next class, history, which we shared with Tim's twin sister, Gabby.

"Hey, Gabby!" I greeted her. "How—"

"What's Tim doing after school tomorrow?" asked Brooke, skipping all pleasantries.

Gabby blinked up at her in confusion. "Uh . . . the same thing as me."

"Which is . . . ?" Brooke leaned forward expectantly, but Gabby leaned back.

"Did Tim not tell you?" she asked.

"Tim *won't* tell us!" Brooke threw her hands in the air. "But he's blowing off all the stuff we have to do for the newspaper."

"Oh." Gabby shook her head. "Well, if Tim's

not telling you, there must be a reason, and I've gotta take his side. Sorry." She mimed sealing her lips.

Brooke looked as if she might explode, so I pulled her away.

"That's okay. Thanks, Gabby!" I squeezed Brooke's arm and said in a low voice, "So his sister knows about it. I'm sure it's fine."

"I guess," said Brooke, but she didn't look satisfied.

After history, I made my way back toward the choir room to ask Miss Thompson a question, when I spotted Stefan and Jeffrey chatting outside the library.

Were they talking about me? I knew it was a long shot, but I lingered just out of sight.

". . . so awesome," Stefan was saying. "Someone started singing 'Penny Wishes,' and then everyone joined in."

Someone? *Someone?*

Me! I wanted to shout. How could he not remember that I started the song if he was so into me?

I leaned against the wall.

Unless he wasn't the one who was into me. Unless it was someone else.

I hadn't won Stefan over . . . yet.

I just had to try a little harder.

CHAPTER

6

Puppy Love

"Well, the nice thing is that a boy out there wants you to go to the dance with him," said Bubbe when I told her about the conversation I'd overheard.

"Yes, but I don't want to go with just any boy. I want to go with Stefan," I said, shoulders sagging. "And he called me 'someone.'"

She patted my leg. "I'm sorry, sweetie. Maybe it wasn't meant to be."

"We don't know that yet," I said, shaking my head. "He accepted my idea for a group date, so there might still be hope."

She tilted her hand from side to side. "And what would be the plan this time?"

"Well, Brooke, Vanessa, and I are going to volunteer at the animal shelter tomorrow, and he'll be taking pictures," I said. "I read somewhere that if you remind a guy of all the nice things you've done together, it creates a positive association."

"You read a lot of things in a lot of places," she said. "But I hope it works out for you."

"Could you give me and my friends a ride to the shelter tomorrow?" I asked.

"For a chance to see the boy who thinks I'm young enough to be your mother?" she asked with a laugh. "Always."

Much to my delight, Bubbe ended up giving my friends, Mary Patrick, *and* Stefan a ride to the shelter. Since the shelter is used to youth volunteers, Mrs. H had left us on our own, which was fine by me. Mary Patrick sat up front next to Bubbe, and Stefan squeezed in next to me.

"Hope you don't mind," he said.

"Mind? Never!" I said with a high-pitched giggle. Someone thumped me on the back of the head, and I stopped. "You know what this reminds me of? The time we went to photograph butterflies."

Stefan squinted as if he were racking his brain, so I added, "The butterfly enclosure was so packed that you had to take pictures with your arm around my shoulder."

"Oh, right!" he said with a laugh. "Those were some of the best photos I've ever taken."

I wiggled in my seat to face him better. "And remember those little cups of nectar they gave us to attract the butterflies?"

"Aw, I'll bet you're sweet enough without the nectar." He smiled at me.

"That's exactly what you said then, too!"

I laughed and looked around at my friends. "Exactly."

"Neat!" said Brooke. But when Stefan wasn't looking, she mouthed, *Tone it down* and made a gesture of lowering her hand.

I blushed and asked, "So how did those photos turn out from the clothing donation center?"

Stefan gave a thumbs-up. "It's going to be hard to choose."

"I can help you pick if you'd like," I told him. "Remember when I started singing 'Penny Wishes,' and everyone joined in?"

"That was awesome," he said.

We pulled up in front of the shelter, and we all thanked her as we climbed out of the car.

"I'll be back in a couple hours," Bubbe told me. "Have fun!" She winked, and in a quieter voice added, "And good luck."

I winked too and headed for the entrance,

but Mary Patrick pulled me back.

"Are you okay?" she asked.

"Of course!" I said with a laugh. "Why?"

"You keep asking Stefan if he remembers things, like you think he caught amnesia."

I could feel myself start to blush, but did my best to fight it. "Do I? Weird."

Then I walked into the building without another word.

Brooke, Vanessa, and Stefan were already signing the volunteer clipboard, and the head volunteer was passing out instruction sheets.

"You'll only be working with the animals that have been cleared for adoption," she said. "So we can avoid any safety issues."

"Tim's going to be disappointed," said Brooke.

The head volunteer smiled at Mary Patrick and me. "Good afternoon, ladies. Thank you for coming. I'm Desiree. If you could please sign in and review the instructions, the fun can begin."

The "fun" included cleaning out the kennels (Vanessa slipped in pee twice) and feeding the animals their supper (Brooke tried a bite of kibble and declared *that* to be the worst thing she'd ever eaten). Then came the best part of all: taking the dogs out of their kennels and playing with them.

The shelter had several fenced-in areas for the dogs to run around, and we each took a dog to a different one, except for Brooke, who went to spend time with the cats. My charge was a floppy-eared mutt named Tinkerbell, who raced around the inside barriers, barking and jumping. It took her a few minutes to calm down and return to me, but once she did, she gave slobbery kisses and kept trying to sit in my lap, even though she was almost my size.

"How many volunteers do you have working here?" I asked Desiree between Tinkerbell's puppy kisses.

"Not as many people as there are animals

who need attention," she said. "We've got about eighty dogs, thirty cats, and twelve volunteers."

"Wow. You'd think more people would want to help out. They're all so cute!" I said to Tinkerbell, who answered with another kiss.

Vanessa wandered over with a pit bull on a leash. "How long does it take for them to get adopted?"

"It depends," said Desiree. "Some stay here longer than others just because of their breed. Like Chester"—she nodded to the pit bull— "and the longer they stay here, the older they get, which makes people want them less."

"What if"—Vanessa put her hands over Chester's ears—"nobody wants him?"

Desiree smiled. "Chester's safe. We run a no-kill facility, so the animals will never be put to sleep. They'll simply live out their days at the shelter."

"Doesn't that take up space?" asked Mary

Patrick. We all looked at her in horror, and she held up her hands. "Not that I'm saying they should be put to sleep!"

"It does take up space," agreed Desiree, "which is why a lot of the friendlier dogs end up sharing kennels. And sometimes we run special deals to help the animals get adopted more quickly."

Mary Patrick glanced around and whistled at Stefan. "Hey, Stefan! When you're done taking selfies with your new best friend, why don't you take some photos of the facility?"

Stefan lowered his camera and scowled, but grabbed his dog's leash and headed for the gate. "Come on, Princess!"

The rest of us followed him in with our own dogs and walked over to the cat habitat to meet Brooke. She was sitting inside one of the floor-to-ceiling cages with a kitten in her hoodie pouch, one on her shoulder, and a fat cat in her lap while she dangled a string for a fourth one.

"Guys!" She beamed up at us. "I'm going to adopt!"

Vanessa and I smiled at each other.

"Which one?" asked Mary Patrick.

"All of them!" she said with a crazy cat lady look in her eye.

"Um . . . maybe talk to your parents first?" I suggested as Stefan snapped a photo of Brooke with all her kitties.

After a lot of coaxing over the phone, Brooke's parents agreed to let her have *one* and told her they could come back and pick it up the next day.

Brooke glanced around. "It's just so hard to choose!"

She finally settled on the tabby in her hoodie pouch, which I'm pretty sure she would've tried to sneak out the door if Desiree hadn't reached for her.

"Don't let anyone else get their hands on

Chelsea," said Brooke. She paused. "Is it okay if I rename her?"

Chelsea Football Club was Brooke's favorite soccer team, and at least the name fit. I've heard her mention a team called Liverpool. That would've given any kitten a complex.

"Of course. And I promise she's all yours," said Desiree.

"So other than coming and working at the shelter, how can kids help?" I asked.

"Adopt," Desiree said simply. "And we always welcome donations of new toys and unopened bags of food."

We thanked her for her time, signed out, and went outside to wait for my grandmother.

"That was fun," I said. "I'm glad the animals have someone to watch over them."

"And if they don't, Brooke can always smuggle them home in her clothing," said Vanessa.

"Why do you think I wore this hoodie?"

asked Brooke, wiggling her eyebrows.

"Too bad Tim had to miss it," I said.

"Don't worry, we'll be sure to rub it in his face," said Brooke with an evil cackle.

And that's just what she did.

The next day in Journalism, Brooke went on and on about how adorable the animals were and showed Tim picture after picture of the cats, including a photo of her and Chelsea that she'd turned into a screensaver.

"Meh." Tim shrugged. "I'm not really into cats."

"What about this?" asked Vanessa, holding out her own cell phone.

"Aww, puppies!" cried Tim, taking it from her.

"How did I ever become friends with you people?" Brooke asked, shaking her head.

Mrs. H called for attention at the front and reminded everyone that since it was Friday, all newspaper submissions were due.

"Okay, does everyone have their stuff for the column?" asked Brooke.

"And for the website?" I added.

"Yes," said Tim and Vanessa.

"Let's hear what we've got for the paper," said Brooke, pointing at Tim.

"'Dear Lincoln's Letters,'" he said, "'how can I get my new boyfriend to be friends with my ex-boyfriend?'"

Brooke snorted. "Even I know that's a bad idea."

He nodded. "My response was 'You can't. Since you once saw your ex as special, they are now destined to be mortal enemies forever. Or until you and your current boyfriend break up.'"

Brooke, Vanessa, and I laughed.

"Vanessa?" Brooke asked.

"Well, since you guys wouldn't let me direct that girl to Katie and me for a makeover"—she made a face—"I went with a different question. This girl wanted to know if she's too young to start plucking her eyebrows."

"Ouch!" said Brooke.

"I told her to check with her parents first," said Vanessa, "and if they're okay with it, then she should have a professional do it the first time, and after that, she'd know where to pluck."

"Good idea," I said. "The last thing we want is to be responsible for some girl plucking out her eyebrows."

Brooke snapped her fingers. "Actually, that's a good rule in general. Tell readers to check with their parents before making any drastic decisions. Tim?"

"On it," he said, pulling out the rule book.

"Heather, what about the dance—"

"I'm not ready!" I cried.

". . . advice?" finished Brooke, giving me a weird look.

I relaxed and felt my cheeks warm. "Sorry. I'm still researching, and I'll put the answer on the website next week. But I have another question that I answered." I fumbled in my backpack for my notebook, and at the same time a small notepad came flying out. The S Files.

I reached for it, but someone walking down the aisle kicked the notepad ahead of them, and it stopped by Stefan's desk.

"No!" I turned to my friends. "Guys, that's a special notepad where I've been gathering intel on Stefan!"

"Intel," said Brooke with a nod. "Nice."

I nudged her. "Do something!"

But at that moment Stefan looked down, saw the notepad, and picked it up.

"My life . . . is over." I covered my face with my hands.

"Shh." Tim pulled at my arms. "Put your hands down. Act normal."

I did what he said, even as Stefan flipped to the front page. "Whose is this?" he asked, looking at us.

"Vanessa's," said Tim, prodding her in the back.

"Right, that's mine!" She jumped out of her seat and snatched it from Stefan, hopefully before he could get to the pages with *Mrs. Heather Marshall* scrawled on them.

"You've been keeping tabs on me?" he asked with a raised eyebrow. "There's a whole list of stuff that I like in there: playing guitar, Indian food, Thunder Barrel . . ."

"You mean a whole list of stuff *Gil* likes," said Vanessa, gazing at Gil adoringly. "Isn't that right, Gil?"

Gil, who was sketching a scorpion for the horoscope, glanced up. "Huh?"

Stefan walked over. "No way, you play guitar too?"

Gil played drums, but the pleading look in Vanessa's eyes made him nod. "Yep. I love that ax."

"We should totally jam together," said Stefan.

"Sure?" said Gil, looking at Vanessa, who nodded subtly. "Sure. Although I'm better on drums."

"That's fine," said Stefan. "Only one of us can be the star of the show, am I right?" He elbowed Gil and chuckled.

Gil smiled and gestured to Vanessa. "Uh . . . whatever she says."

"Cool. Later!" Stefan wandered back to his desk, and Vanessa handed the notepad to me.

"Thank you, thank you, thank you," I gushed, quickly stashing it back in my bag. "I will totally start leaving it at home."

"No," said Brooke. "You'll burn it because you won't need it anymore. Not with me in charge!"

"Uh-oh," said Vanessa as Brooke leaned forward.

"Tonight, the four of us are meeting at my place," she said in a low voice. "Heather, I'm sorry, but as good as you are with other people's love lives, you're terrible at your own."

"Fair point," I said.

"So I'm going to come up with a plan to get you and Stefan together. And it starts with *Stealing Ever After*."

7

Operation HAHA

I wasn't sure what to expect at Brooke's house that evening, but it definitely wasn't to be greeted at the door by my best friend wearing a stern-looking military cap and one of her dad's business coats.

"Schwartz!" she greeted me. "Good to see you. Jackson and Antonides are already inside."

"Really? We're going with last names?" I asked.

"Extreme times call for extreme measures," she informed me, turning on her heel. "If you'll come with me, everyone else is assembled in the war room."

"The war room?" I repeated, following her into the kitchen.

All the lights were out except the one above the dining table, illuminating a large sheet of paper. Vanessa and Tim stood at one end with markers in hand, playing tic-tac-toe on a blank corner.

"Guys!" Brooke took their markers. "This is serious business."

"'Operation HAHA'?" I asked, reading the top of the paper.

She grinned. "It stands for 'Heather, Ask Him Already'!"

I rolled my eyes.

"Can we get started?" asked Tim. "Operation HAHA is conflicting with Operation Tim Has a Life."

Brooke nodded. "Now that Angel's here, we can begin."

"Angel?" I repeated.

"Code name," she said. "That's you."

"No code names," said Vanessa, shaking her head. "It's too confusing."

"But I made a whole list!" Brooke held up a clipboard.

"No!" the rest of us chorused.

Brooke pouted. "Fine. I suppose code phrases are out too." She tossed the clipboard aside. "But for the record, 'The angel is in heaven' was going to mean the mission was accomplished."

I frowned. "That sounds more like I died."

Brooke bit her lip. "You may have a point. Okay, let's get down to business." She stood near the middle of the table. "I've done—"

"Wait, I need something to drink first," said Vanessa, reaching for a bottle of soda.

"No drinks near the map!" said Brooke.

"Unless it's out of a canteen," added Tim.

Vanessa and I snickered.

"Guys, let's focus!" Brooke smacked the table with a spatula. We all jumped.

"What's that for?" I asked.

"It's my pointer." She held it up. "My parents wouldn't loan me money for a real one."

"And all this time we thought Mary Patrick was weird," said Tim, shaking his head.

"Just . . . come closer," said Brooke.

Tim, Vanessa, and I looked at one another and then shuffled toward the table. We stood around the paper, which turned out to be a birds'-eye view of a movie theater.

"I've done some online reconnaissance before our mission. Here's the layout of the theater." She tapped the map with her spatula. "According to Pete, who works the ticket stand, the theater for Saturday's matinee is currently at twenty percent occupancy, which means several people have already bought advanced tickets." She paced at one end of the table. "I read in a recent finance magazine that early ticket buyers tend to go for an optimum viewing experience, which would place them here." She drew an X with a black marker over a section of seats in the middle of the theater.

"You have time to research money magazines, contact movie theater people, and come up with terrible code words," said Tim, "but you can't be bothered to read classic literature?"

"Silence!" Brooke whacked her spatula against her palm. "Ow!"

She winced, shaking the pain out of her hand. "Now, more than likely, the majority of people going on a Saturday afternoon will be the elderly, parents with young kids, or people looking for a deal."

"A deal?" I raised an eyebrow.

"Matinees cost less than evening tickets. Everyone knows that," said Brooke. "Stay on top of the game, Schwartz."

I saluted her.

"The elderly will sit in the front because they're practically blind," said Brooke, pointing to a section near the screen. "Those with young kids will sit on the ends because at some point there will be a restroom break or tantrum. All we have to do is get there before the people who are looking for a deal. Make sense?"

"None of this makes sense," said Tim. "But go on."

"More than likely, everyone in our group is going to want to sit in the back." Brooke pointed to a section marked "Back." "So we need to ensure that Heather and Stefan sit together, which means they need to enter the theater at roughly the same pace." She pointed her spatula at Vanessa. "Which is where you come in."

Vanessa's eyes lit up. "Ooh! Do I get to drop from the ceiling in a harness? Set up a diversion using fireworks?" She slammed her palms on the table and leaned forward. "Something that requires a costume change?"

Brooke backed up a step and blinked. "I like your enthusiasm, but no. You're going to make small talk with Heather just inside the entrance to the theater." She reached into a plastic tub beside her and pulled out some checkers with labels on them, placing "Heather" and "Vanessa" just outside the entrance to the theater.

"Oh," said V, slumping her shoulders. "Well . . . I can at least wear a flashy hat."

"That's probably safer than fireworks," I said with a nod. "But, Brooke, if V and I are talking to each other, what if we miss Stefan?"

She smiled triumphantly and held up a third checker. "That's what Gil is for! He'll stand with you and watch for Stefan." She added the Gil checker and held the Stefan checker in her hand. "As soon as Gil sees Stefan enter the theater"— she put the checker down—"he alerts Vanessa and Heather, so they can slowly walk toward the theater, 'accidentally' bumping into Stefan."

"What if Stefan has other people with him?" I asked.

"That's where I come in," said Brooke, pulling out another checker. "I'll run interference to block off whoever's with Stefan, so he's forced to go in by himself. Then you guys will hold back just a little bit, so he can sit first." She moved Stefan's checker to a seat. "And then Heather will follow, with Vanessa and Gil behind her."

"That's perfect!" I said, clapping my hands.

"But what if some cute girl comes to sit on his other side?" asked Tim.

Brooke, Vanessa, and I all turned to stare at him, and he blinked back at us.

"What?" He thought for a beat and said, "Oh!

No, Heather's cute. I meant some other cute girl who's not nearly as cute."

"Nice save," said Vanessa, patting him on the back.

"Believe it or not, I actually planned for female anomalies," said Brooke, taking out another checker. "Tim, you'll get to the theater earlier and lurk in the shadows."

"That doesn't sound like I'll get kicked out at all," he mumbled.

"And if another girl approaches Stefan, you'll act as a decoy and draw her attention. Then if the empty seat next to Stefan stays open, you'll slide in and take it."

She placed the checker in her hand on the paper. "Decoy."

"That doesn't say *decoy*, " said Tim, squinting at it. "That says *dummy*."

Brooke glanced down too. "Does it? Well, either way, I was thinking of you the whole time." She smiled at him, then pointed her spatula at me. "Heather! For small talk, what do you have?"

I sat up straight. "Um. Remember when—"

"Stop!" Brooke shook her head. "Remember when you wouldn't stop saying 'remember when'? It's time to focus on his future. With you!" She reached into her plastic tub again and pulled out some index cards. "Here are some questions to consider."

I read the top card. "'Hey, Stefan, you're pretty smart. Would you help me with my science homework?'" I lowered the card. "But science is one of my best subjects. I could probably help him with his."

"Science is just an example. You can switch it out for something else that you need help with. But this way you're (a) paying him a compliment," she said, counting off on her fingers, "(b) letting him feel important by helping you, and (c) arranging a future date."

Tim whistled through his teeth. "Brooke is actually encouraging a girl to ask a guy for help?"

"It was Abel's idea." She made a face. "I promised I'd include some of his suggestions."

"Wait." I held up a hand. "So Abel knows that I have a crush on Stefan?"

She shook her head. "Of course not! I used fake names. He won't figure it out." She paused. "Well, he might figure it out. He's pretty smart."

I read the next question out loud. "'Can I tell you a secret?'"

Brooke smiled. "I came up with that one. It gives him a reason to lean in close, and there's that shared connection of personal info."

"But I also have to tell him a secret," I said with a frown.

"It doesn't have to be a big secret," said Vanessa. "Tell him about your fear of sprinklers."

"You guys!" I jerked my head toward Tim,

who was grinning from ear to ear.

"Nah, that secret isn't juicy enough. How about some bigger ones?" he suggested.

Vanessa punched his arm and asked me, "What are you going to wear?"

I was prepared for this. "His favorite color is green, so I've got a green sweater with silver leaves that . . . what?"

All three of my friends wore disgusted expressions.

"But I haven't even gotten to the best part," I insisted. "The leaves make tinkling noises when they rustle!"

Brooke snapped her fingers in the air, and Vanessa reached for a binder on the counter, flipping it open on the kitchen table.

"I'm thinking skinny jeans with riding boots and a green tunic blouse with a nice, chunky belt." She showed me a sketch before flipping to another page. "We'll braid your hair first and then pin it up in a bun."

I flipped the pages back and forth. "That looks amazing."

"Only because you'll be wearing it," she said with a smile. "I've got the blouse and boots, and you own the jeans, right?"

I nodded.

Vanessa snapped the binder shut. "I'll come by your house before the movie, so we can get your look together." She paused. "And maybe go through your closet to get rid of musical sweaters."

True to her word, Vanessa was outside my place the next morning with a garment bag and her styling tote.

"FYI, you're pretty special to get a house call," she teased when I let her in. "Only A-listers can afford my usual fee."

"Why do you think I shared my peanut butter

sandwich with you when we were six?" I asked. "I knew it would pay off someday."

At the sound of our voices, my mom poked her head out of the living room.

"Hello, Vanessa dear, how are you? Have you had breakfast?"

"Yes, Mrs. Schwartz," she said. She held up her beauty tote. "I just came to prep Heather for her da—"

"Daytime movie with my classmates!" I grabbed V's waist and nudged her upstairs. "So exciting. Let's go!"

V raised an eyebrow at me as we climbed the stairs, and I shook my head. "Only Bubbe knows," I whispered.

"Gotcha."

When we got up to my room, Vanessa hung her garment bag on my doorknob and pulled out my desk chair, gesturing to it with a flourish.

"Welcome to Vantastic Hair Salon," she said.

I smiled and took a seat. "Will this take long or be painful?"

"Nah," she said. "You brush your hair, unlike Brooke. I tried to braid hers once and had to stop every couple minutes to pick out a knot. It's like she's never heard of conditioner."

I giggled and settled back.

"Are you excited about today?" asked V.

"I think more nervous than anything," I said. "Whenever one of us comes up with a clever scheme, something usually goes wrong."

She grinned and brushed my hair. "Yeah, but if it's meant to be, it'll all work out."

"Yeah," I said vaguely.

For some reason, V's words didn't cheer me. It felt like things *hadn't* been working out. I'd been putting in a ton of effort and getting zero results.

"Are you okay?" she asked, stopping mid-brush.

I smiled and nodded. "Of course. How are

things going for you and Katie?" I asked. "Have you had any interest in your makeover services?"

"Oh, loads!" said Vanessa, with a huge grin. "We've got half the day booked already. Seven sessions each!"

"Wow! That's a lot of customers," I said while she walked around behind me.

"And a lot of clothing donations," she added, sweeping my hair back. I felt her pause with my hair in her hands. "Katie's a little upset that we're not making money, though."

I tilted my head back and glanced at her upside down. "You're doing the right thing."

"I know. And I would've just spent the money on more clothes. Or a puppy to put in my purse."

I giggled. "You're definitely doing the right thing."

After a few more minutes, Vanessa backed away, circling my chair to survey her work. "Beautiful. Go check it out!"

I went to the bathroom mirror and marveled at the masterpiece she'd created with just hair. My hair.

"V, it's gorgeous!" I turned to her. "Could you do it again for the actual dance?"

"You get this date, and it's a deal," she said, extending her hand.

We shook on it.

A half hour later, Bubbe was pulling her car up to the curb outside the movie theater with me and Vanessa inside.

"You're sure you want to go through with this?" she asked me.

I nodded. "If nothing else, I'll enjoy the movie."

"Then here." Bubbe took my hand and slapped something in it. "For good luck, just in case."

It was a charm with the *hamsa* on it, a flat hand with the thumb and pinkie pointing out, meant to ward off the evil eye.

"Oh, and this." She plopped a marble painted like a blue eye into my palm.

"Is that real?" Vanessa looked a little pale.

"No, it's for protection. It'll be a dark theater," I said. "I don't think the evil eye will be able to see me."

"You can never be too sure," she said.

"Well, thanks." I pocketed the items, along with some cash she gave me for snacks, and gave her a peck on the cheek.

"Have fun, girls!" She waved to me and Vanessa when we got out. Then she drove away.

"And now . . ." Vanessa rubbed her hands together. "It begins!"

CHAPTER

8

Movie Mayhem

V and I bought our tickets and walked into the lobby, where a group of kids from Journalism stood around talking, including Brooke and Tim. Brooke waved when she saw us, but I pointed to the concession stand. There was no way I was walking into the theater without fresh popcorn. It was the perfect bravery booster. Also, it was delicious.

"I'm going to join them," Vanessa told me. "Hurry, okay? Oh, and could you please get me some M&M's?" She tried to hand me money, but I nudged it away.

"I've got it. It's the least I can do," I told her, and hurried toward the shortest line.

While I waited for the guy to put my order together, I glanced toward the entrance, watching for Stefan. When he came in wearing jeans and a green sweater, I almost fainted.

He was so dreamy. How could I have let my friends talk me out of *my* green sweater? Then Stefan and I could've matched!

I was debating the creepiness level of snapping a pic with my phone when the concession guy put the last item of my order on the counter.

Buttery, hot popcorn.

I leaned forward and took a deep breath, handing him my money. After he gave me the change, I tucked the money and the M&M's in my coat pocket and tried to balance my popcorn and soda while grabbing napkins and a straw.

"Here, let me help."

I glanced up as Emmett Elders draped a

handful of napkins over my popcorn.

"Emmett! Hi!" I nodded at my popcorn. "And thanks!"

He shrugged and smiled. "It'll keep it warm."

"What are you doing here?" I asked. "Did you join the newspaper?"

"The newspaper?" he repeated, then looked around and saw the group of us huddled together. "Oh . . . no. I'm here to see a movie with my family."

"Right." I blushed. "Because regular people go to the movies too."

"It's not just a rumor," he said with a smirk. "What are you here to see?"

"*Stealing Ever After*," I said. With a sheepish grin, I added, "For the second time. Have you seen it?"

He shook his head. "Is it good?"

I held up two fingers, smiling. "Second time."

It was his turn to blush. "Ha! Duh."

"What are you seeing?"

He cleared his throat and in a softer voice said, "Um . . . *Fluffy Monkeys Go Bananas?*"

I couldn't help the laugh that escaped. Or the echo it made off the walls.

"It's not my choice!" he said, crossing his heart. "My little sister—"

"Heather!" Brooke called my name, and I almost dropped my popcorn. She beckoned for me, and I could see Stefan standing right beside her.

My stomach flipped.

Showtime!

"I'm sorry, Emmett. I've got to go," I told him. "But enjoy your . . . fluffy monkeys." I swallowed a laugh.

He grinned and waved as I walked as fast as I could without losing a precious kernel of popcorn. I handed Vanessa her candy and took my place next to Brooke.

"Do I look okay?" I whispered to her while Stefan had his back turned.

She nodded. "Start walking. I'll get Stefan in motion."

But no sooner had she said that than he started walking in on his own. A couple other kids followed after, taking what was supposed to be *my* place behind him.

I looked to Brooke. "Do something!" I whispered.

"Uh . . . hey, did someone drop a dollar?" she asked loudly, pulling one from her pocket and throwing it on the carpet.

Stefan and the others kept walking, but a complete stranger bent over and picked up the money. "Yep, that was mine! Thanks!"

"But . . ." Brooke watched him head for the concession stand. Then she turned to me. "You owe me a dollar."

"I got this," said Vanessa, cramming a handful

of candy into her mouth and grabbing my arm. "Look out! Coming through!" She tugged me toward the theater, bumping people aside with her hips until we'd squeezed right behind Stefan.

"Dude! What gives?" asked a boy we'd cut off.

She looked him up and down. "You want to see this princess movie more than we do?"

He instantly grew quiet.

I leaned close to Vanessa. "You know you've strayed completely from Brooke's original operation."

"Yeah." She poured some more candy into her palm. "I thought it was time for Plan V."

We both giggled.

Vanessa shifted so I was in front of her, and soon Stefan and I were sitting side by side, me on the left and him on the right.

"Hey," he said, giving me a nod.

"Hi," I said, putting my soda in the holder

between us. If he accidentally took a sip? I'd be okay with that.

Tim came in from the opposite side to fill the other seat next to Stefan, and Brooke sat behind my right shoulder.

Once we were settled, Stefan kicked his feet up on the seat in front of him, and I did the same.

"Nice boots," he said.

To my other side, Vanessa twisted in her seat and said, "Thanks! I got them—"

An orange Skittle beaned her on the side of the head.

"Owww!" She glared at Brooke. "What . . ."

Brooke must have made some sort of gesture, because V's eyes widened, and then she smiled indulgently at Stefan.

"I mean . . . *Heather* got them at a close-out sale."

"I just love to shop!" I added.

Stefan smiled and nodded, then pulled out his phone.

Brooke prodded my seat and whispered, "Bring him back to you!"

Apparently, she was louder than she thought because Stefan turned to look at her. "What?"

Even I looked at Brooke to see how she was going to explain that one.

"Uh . . ." Brooke's eyes shifted from side to side. "It's a cheer! Bring it back, bring it back, waaaay back!" She rolled her arms and threw them out in a V.

Tim snorted.

"I didn't picture you as a spirit squad kind of girl," said Stefan, grinning.

I touched his arm to divert his attention. "So are you excited about the movie?"

He shrugged and faced front again. "I guess. I've seen it, so . . ."

This time, Brooke pretended to tie her shoe

and whispered, "Ask if he wants some popcorn or Coke."

I turned to Stefan. "Want some popcoke?"

Tim snickered, then quickly switched to "Ow!" as Brooke flicked the back of his head.

Stefan wrinkled his forehead. "Sorry?"

"I meant do you want some popcorn?" I asked, holding out my bag.

"Sure!" he said.

Instead of plucking out a few pieces and savoring each bite like I do, he formed his hand into a scoop and smushed the contents against his face. Only about half the pieces made it into his mouth. He chewed twice and swallowed.

I winced. "Doesn't that hurt going down?"

"Nah," he said. "One time I swallowed a piece of cactus. That hurt."

"Seriously?" I asked with a laugh. "Were you stranded in the desert?"

"I was stranded at my cousin's house," he

said. "They don't have TV, so we entertained ourselves by daring one another to eat things." He took a swig of my soda. "What's the weirdest thing you ever ate?"

Stefan was asking me about myself! That had never happened before. I wanted to turn to my friends and squeal and jump.

"Oh!" I thought for a moment. "Um . . . probably calves' feet," I said.

Stefan almost spit soda in his lap. "For real?"

I nodded and smiled at the impressed look on his face. "It's called *ptcha*. I had it when I was really little."

Brooke poked my arm again and whispered, "Invite him to have some!"

"You want to try it sometime?" I asked.

He shook his head and laughed. "No, but I'll have some more popcorn."

"Sure!" I held out the bag, and he dove in.

When he withdrew his hand, I realized

almost half the popcorn was gone.

"Whoops," he said, peering down. "Sorry."

"No problem! I'll get a refill before the movie starts," I said.

Vanessa stood up so I could get past and tugged the hem of my tunic, flashing me a thumbs-up.

I poured the last of my old popcorn in the garbage and carried the bag to the concession stand.

"Could I get a refill, please?" I asked. "The freshest batch you've got, with lots of butter." My eye traveled to a vat of cheese. "Ooh, and some nachos!"

"Sure thing." The concession worker took my bag and filled it to the brim, dousing the whole thing in butter. He placed it on the counter in front of me, and I breathed deeply while he made the nachos. "That'll be thirteen fifty," he said when he was done.

I reached into my pocket and pulled out some

bills and the blue eyeball Bubbe had given me.

"Sorry. You probably don't want this, do you?" I joked, handing over the bills and holding on to the eyeball.

"I've been offered stranger things," the guy assured me with a chuckle. "Be right back with your change."

I rested my elbows on the counter around my popcorn bag and rolled the eyeball between my hands, staring into space.

Tim's face popped up next to mine.

"Gah!" I dropped the eyeball into my popcorn.

"What the heck are you doing?" asked Tim.

"Getting some more popcorn before the movie," I said, taking my change from the concession stand worker. "Stefan really likes it."

"Stefan . . ." Tim shook his head. "Don't you see anything wrong with this picture?"

I grabbed a handful of napkins. "I should've gotten a bigger bag?"

"No! You shouldn't have gotten *any* popcorn while he sits on his butt. He should've offered to get it for you. Emmett isn't even in our same theater and I saw him help you!"

I jiggled the popcorn down a bit. "But if Stefan got up to get the popcorn, he might have decided to sit somewhere else when he got back."

Tim sighed and ran a hand through his hair. "Then...Heather...that's a pretty good sign he doesn't like you."

As hard as I tried, I couldn't keep the scowl off my face. "What's your problem? Don't you want me to be happy?"

"Yes!" Tim threw his hands in the air. "And trust me, it's not gonna be with Stefan. You want to go out with someone who will make you happy? Try someone you have more in common with."

I stared at him.

"Who whistles the same tune," he said.

I blinked.

"Who sings the same song," he tried again.

"Stefan and I sang—"

"I'm talking about Emmett!" Tim said, and then quickly lowered his voice. "You're in choir together, you're in the same grade, you probably even have some of the same classes."

"But he's not Stefan," I countered.

"Stefan isn't that great."

I rolled my eyes. "Look, I know that you're jealous of him and how he gets the better sports stories, but you need to get over it because"—I shrugged—"I'm not getting over him."

Without another word, I picked up my food and walked toward the theater.

"Wow," said Tim to my retreating back.

"He's seriously changing you."

"Only for the better," I called over my shoulder.

By the time I opened the theater door, the lights had dimmed and the previews were rolling. I picked my way down the aisle and took my seat next to Stefan, who smiled.

"I was starting to worry something had happened to you," he said.

"You were?" A warm glow filled my chest.

He nodded. "And I should've asked if you wanted me to get the refill. Since I ate, like, half the bag."

"Oh, it's no big deal." I settled back in my seat, smiling smugly at Tim, who had come in behind me.

The last preview ended, and the theater got quiet except for the sounds of people rustling popcorn bags and shaking candy out of boxes. And then the film opened with Snow White,

Cinderella, and Sleeping Beauty battling a two-headed ogre.

"Yaaay," I cheered quietly and tilted the popcorn bag so Stefan could get some.

"What the—" He squinted and gazed into the container.

"What's wrong?" I asked.

"There's something in here." He fished his phone out of his pocket, turned it on, and held it over the popcorn.

"Oh no," I whispered.

The eyeball.

Stefan screamed. A high-pitched, blood-freezing scream.

"Calm down," said Tim, not taking his eyes off the screen. "The ogre's not real."

Stefan leaped to his feet. "There are body parts in the popcorn!" He knocked the bag out of my hand. "Don't eat that!"

"But it's—"

Everyone around us had switched their attention from the movie to Stefan.

I turned to Tim and winced. "I accidentally dropped my *bubbe*'s evil eye charm in the popcorn!"

An expression of delight crossed his face, and I jabbed a finger at him.

"Don't laugh!"

Stefan lunged over his seat toward Brooke and threw her bag on the ground. "Put it down!" She quickly tried to cram the handful she was holding into her mouth, but Stefan unclenched her fingers and shook the pieces loose.

"Hey!"

"We have to tell the manager!" He gripped my arm, and I glanced up at him dreamily.

We had to tell the manager. Together.

Tim shoved me from behind, and I snapped out of it.

Right! There was a crisis. Stefan was already

running for the exit, so my friends and I hurried after him. Gil was faster than any of us, and by the time we caught up to him and Stefan, Gil had pushed Stefan into a corner and was talking to him in a low voice.

"It was in the popcorn!" Stefan was telling him.

"Dude, calm down. It was fake." Gil looked at Vanessa, who held out Bubbe's eyeball charm. "See?"

Instantly, the wild look left Stefan's eyes, and his breathing slowed from racehorse to human. "What?" He snatched it out of Vanessa's hand.

Behind me, someone made a choking sound, and I glanced back. Tim had his lips pressed together and was tearing up from trying not to laugh.

"That's what I've been trying to tell you," I said as Stefan held the eyeball charm up to the light and rotated it. "It's not real."

"But who would've put it in the popcorn?" he asked.

And then Tim couldn't hold it in any longer. Between fits of laughter, he said, "I totally should've recorded that and put it online! Would've gone viral in five seconds!"

Stefan's lip curled. "*You* did this?"

He drew back both arms and shoved Tim hard into the wall.

"Stefan!" I shouted.

Vanessa and Brooke gasped.

Tim's face turned an angry red, and he charged forward. "Dude! What's your problem?"

He emphasized the last word with a shove of his own, but unlike him, Stefan didn't have a wall to fall against. Instead, Stefan stumbled back, hands clutching at the air before he landed on his butt in an unceremonious heap.

It was so quiet you could hear a pin drop. Or a Stefan.

We all stared down at him. So did several passersby.

I finally stepped forward to help, but Stefan was already scrambling to his feet to have another go at Tim.

Gil jumped between them, throwing out both his arms. "Okay, just stop. Both of you! Stefan, you're older than he is." He turned to Tim. "And you're stronger. Both of you should know better."

Stefan and Tim glared at each other, but neither of them moved.

"I was only defending myself," huffed Tim. "He shouldn't have attacked me."

"You deserved it," said Stefan through clenched teeth.

"Why, because I laughed at you?" Tim demanded. "Bro, you've got a lot of fights in your future if you can't handle that."

"You didn't just laugh," Stefan snapped. "You set me up by planting this thing." He flung the evil eye at Tim, and Tim lunged at him, but Gil held him back.

"I didn't do that!" shouted Tim.

"No?" Stefan held his arms open. "Then who did?"

I could've stepped forward at that moment and defended Tim. I could've admitted my part in it so they could shake hands and we could go back to the movie.

But things were going so well between me and Stefan, and I didn't want to ruin it.

So I stayed quiet.

And Tim stared at me for a moment, a hurt look in his eyes before he sighed and said, "I guess we'll never know."

I mouthed the words *thank you* to him, but he just turned and walked away.

9

Math to the Rescue

"So do you think I've blown my chances with Stefan?" I asked Brooke and Vanessa.

The three of us were sitting on my living room floor, eating melty slices of pizza out of a grease-stained box. A few hours had passed since the scene at the movie theater. Luckily, most of the people had ignored Stefan's outburst and gone back to watching the show, except for Tim, who'd left early, and Stefan, who decided to go for a walk to cool off.

He wouldn't even look at us once he realized

the eyeball was a fake, no doubt embarrassed by his freak-out.

Now, during Musketeer Movies night, it was all I could think about.

My two best friends gave each other an uneasy look before Brooke cleared her throat.

"I think the bigger question is . . . why do you still want to date him?" she asked. "He's crazy and violent, a combination that only works in wrestling."

"It wasn't his fault," I said. "I was the one who accidentally dropped the eyeball in the popcorn."

"Weird." Vanessa leaned back and studied me. "You didn't seem to remember that earlier when Tim took the blame."

I picked an olive off my pizza. "I know. Do you think he hates me now?"

"I don't think Tim could ever hate you," said

Brooke. "But I think he's pretty upset that you didn't stick up for him."

I nodded. "I'll tell him I'm sorry on Monday."

"And what about Stefan?" asked Vanessa. "The dance is next weekend, you know."

"I say again," said Brooke. She leaned close to me. "He's crazy."

I scoffed. "If by crazy you mean brave, saving us all from human-flavored popcorn, then I agree." My argument was thinner than the pizza crust I was holding, but it didn't matter. "After what happened, though, he probably won't even talk to me anymore." I lowered my plate and sighed.

"Especially not once everyone in school finds out," added Vanessa. I raised my eyebrow at her, and she winced. "Sorry! But it's true."

She was right, of course. During Stefan and Tim's scuffle, I'd seen a couple kids from school among the passersby. There was no way word wouldn't get out.

"What I need is to put Stefan in a good mood *and* show him I'm the right girl," I said.

"You could give him a million dollars and have him hypnotized," said Brooke, taking a bite of pizza. "Hypnotists can make people believe *anything*."

Vanessa held up her drink. "Why doesn't Heather take him to the hypnotist first and convince Stefan she already gave him the million dollars?"

Brooke pointed at her. "Better plan." She snapped her fingers. "Oh wait! Can you convince him he's a clown?"

I frowned. "How does that help?"

"It doesn't, but it's funny," she said with a grin.

I rolled my eyes. "Well, I'm not hypnotizing him. I want him to go out with me because he wants to. And if he doesn't . . ." I trailed off as I realized what Tim had been trying to tell me.

"If he doesn't, then he *is* a clown," Brooke announced.

When my friends left, I went in search of the rest of my family, who were playing rummy at the kitchen table.

"Did you have a good day today?" asked my dad. I picked up his cards and looked at them.

"Sort of," I said. "The movies weren't as great as I thought." I pulled the evil eye out of my pocket and slid it across the table to her. "This turned out to be bad luck."

Bubbe raised an eyebrow, but I shook my head.

"You wouldn't believe me if I told you. But Tim's mad at me now."

"Tim Antonides?" Daddy took the cards I was holding and played a couple. "I thought you were thick as thieves."

"We were, but I was a bad friend," I said with

a sigh. "And he's a very good one."

"So fix it," said Mom with a shrug. She played a few cards of her own. "Be a better friend."

"I can't. Not yet."

All three adults looked up at me.

"It's hard to explain," I said. "Tim doesn't want me to do something that I have to do."

My mother peered down her glasses at me, "Heather, are you joining a gang?"

I rolled my eyes. "No, Mom. What gang is a twelve-year-old going to join?"

"There are gangs for everything," she said, tapping her fingernail on the table. "And your father works for some very important people, so we can't afford you on the news for spray-paint shenanigans."

"I'm not going to be on the news," I said. Then I thought about what had happened at the movie theater and quietly prayed, *Please don't let me be on the news.*

While the adults kept playing, I went up to my room and flipped through Vanessa's magazines, hoping to find a solution for both my problem with Tim and my problem with Stefan.

To fix things with Tim, though, I didn't really need any advice. I knew I'd have to apologize and offer to set things straight. But how could I tell Stefan the eyeball in the popcorn had belonged to me without completely repelling him?

An ad next to a magazine article caught my eye. It was for custom desserts with two girls hugging, holding a BFF sugar cookie between them.

Say it with sugar, coaxed the ad.

I pulled out the S Files notepad, checking to see if I'd recorded any type of pastry preference Stefan had.

Nothing.

"Although . . ." I murmured to myself, gazing at my pages and pages of data.

I didn't have to say it with sugar; I could say it with something else. Or rather, a basket full of something elses, including a note asking him to the dance!

I flipped through my notepad from the beginning and, on a separate piece of paper, jotted down ideas that I could turn into small gifts. Then I grabbed the sheet music for "Penny Wishes" and cut out some song lyrics, which I glued to the front of an index card:

The nights grow cold, the nights grow long.

Then on the back:

Will you "fall into winter" with me?
Heather

Now, all I had to do was shop for the gifts, and on Monday . . .

I chewed my lip thoughtfully. How was I going to get the basket to Stefan? Handing it to him wouldn't be romantic or exciting enough. It had to be a magnificent surprise. But something for his eyes only.

Since he was an eighth grader and I was a sixth grader, the only time I was guaranteed to see him was the one class we had together: Journalism. I couldn't just put it on his desk, though. I'd have to hide it somewhere for him to find.

I closed my eyes and pictured the newsroom. Where could I hide a gift basket? Behind Mrs. H's desk, inside a trash can, inside a cabinet . . . But anybody could spot it in those places and take it.

Then I remembered the bookcases that lined the walls. They were filled with old yearbooks, and they were tall . . . so tall only a couple people in class could reach the top shelf. And if I positioned the gift just right, I could make it so it was only visible from a certain location.

I drew a quick diagram of the newsroom and the bookcases, calculating the angle the gift could be seen from that would allow the least visibility to the rest of the class. I'd have to find a way to sneak the gift in and put it on a shelf I normally couldn't reach, but it was a workable plan.

"Thank you, math!" I said, dropping my pencil with a satisfied grin.

There was a knock on my bedroom door, and Bubbe poked her head in. "Doing homework on a Saturday night?"

"Something like that," I said, setting my diagram aside. "What's up?"

"I just wanted to check on you. Especially since this turned out to be bad luck," she said, holding up the evil eye. "Everything okay?"

"Yep," I said. Normally, I would've told her the whole story, but if she knew Stefan had gotten into a fight with Tim, she'd probably do everything in her power to make sure I didn't end up with him.

Bubbe waited in the doorway for me to say more, but when I didn't, she came in and sat beside me on my bed. "This thing you're going to do that Tim doesn't approve of . . . Is it asking Stefan to the dance?"

I sighed. I might not be willing to tell her about my day, but I definitely wasn't going to lie to her. "Yep," I said again, hoping she'd drop it.

"Tim is a good friend," she said. "And a smart kid."

"He is," I agreed. "But I'm smart too, Bubbe."

She smiled at me. "There's an expression: 'Love is blind.'"

I nodded. "Stefan is blind to how much I love him."

She shook her head. "No, honey."

"Stefan is blind to how much he loves me?"

Bubbe leaned forward and kissed my

forehead. "Keep your eyes open, darling. That's all I'm trying to say." She got up and held out the evil eye. "And this wasn't bad luck. I don't know what happened today, but this kept it from being even worse."

I smiled at her. "You're probably right."

She winked at me and closed my bedroom door behind her.

But she was all kinds of wrong. Her charm hadn't helped, and love wasn't blind. In fact, it was about to turn everything around.

"What's with the gym bag?" Bubbe asked on Monday morning as I climbed out of the car. She had taken me to school extra early again, but instead of going to choir, I planned to go to the newsroom.

"Uh . . . just some old clothes I don't wear anymore. We're collecting them at school," I said. Then I shifted the bag behind me so she couldn't see the basket handle pressing against the nylon: Stefan's gift.

She smiled. "You kids today set such good examples."

Yes. We lied to our grandmothers.

I smiled and kissed her cheek before climbing out of the car.

Then I double-timed it to the newsroom. And froze at the door.

Mary Patrick was sitting at her desk reading the latest issue, marker in hand as she circled various lines and muttered to herself.

I had to get her out of the room, and quick before anyone else showed up.

"Hey, Mary Patrick?"

She jumped at the sound of my voice and scowled. "You're here early."

"I have choir," I said. "But Vanessa wanted to see you in the courtyard."

"Vanessa? What for?"

I shrugged. "Probably something fashion related."

Mary Patrick groaned and got to her feet. "This better be good."

I made a big show of checking the advice box, watching her walk down the hall out of the corner of my eye. When I was sure she was far enough away, I bolted into the classroom and dragged a desk over to the bookshelf I'd chosen. I climbed onto the desk and removed an armful of books. Then I reached into the bag on my shoulder and pulled out Stefan's gift basket and my dance invite, kissing the front for good luck. I snuggled the card between an inflatable guitar and a bag of jelly beans and set the whole basket on the shelf.

Dropping back down to the floor, I walked the room, making sure the basket was only visible from one place: the pencil sharpener. Nobody would think to look at the bookshelves while they were trying to sharpen a pencil.

"Perfect," I whispered, dragging the desk I'd used back into place and hiding the yearbooks in a cabinet.

I was halfway to the choir room before Mary Patrick ran into me.

"Vanessa wasn't out there," she informed me.

"Really?" I kept walking. "She must've solved the problem on her own."

"I hope it wasn't about the One Big Happy visit this afternoon," she said with a frown. "I'm already short Tim and Stefan."

That slowed me down. "Neither of them is going?"

"Well, Tim has a thing that he told me about last week, and Stefan texted me yesterday saying he can't make it."

Dread and disappointment filled me.

"Did he say why?" I asked.

"Probably because of what happened at the movies."

My eyes widened. "You know about that?"

Mary Patrick smirked. "I'm the editor of the paper, and half the kids who write for it were there. You really think I wouldn't find out? Plus, Stefan told me himself."

"He did?" I wrung my hands together. "What exactly did he say?"

Her smirk widened into a full smile. "That Tim pranked him and he overreacted."

I felt a twang of guilt but nodded. "Just a little bit."

"Anyway, I'm sure he has no desire to spend time with Tim outside school," she said. "And I don't want them getting into another fight when we're trying to be good examples."

"I guess you have a point," I said, my shoulders sagging a little.

Mary Patrick's forehead wrinkled as she watched my reaction. "It'll be okay. We can handle it without them." She narrowed her eyes. "Or are you upset about something else?"

"Of course not!" I said with my biggest smile. "I'm glad it's just us girls." I glanced down at my wrist. "I should be going. Look at the time!"

"You're not even wearing a watch," she said with a frown.

"See you in Journalism!" I called, speed-walking away.

As soon as I entered the choir room, someone called my name. Emmett was standing with Jeffrey and a couple other guys, waving me over. Emmett wore his usual cheerful smile, and my spirits lifted a little.

"Hi, guys!" I said.

"Word around campus is that you had an interesting time at the movies," he said as I got closer.

I slowed down. "Define interesting," I said evasively.

Emmett turned to Jeffrey and the other guys, and I was treated to a reenactment of what had happened in the theater. Unfortunately, it was embarrassingly accurate.

"Body parts in the popcorn!" One of the guys threw his hands in the air and ran around. "Don't eat that!" He pretended to knock something out of Emmett's hand. Then he and Jeffrey got into a shoving match while the other guys tried to break them up. When they finished, everyone was cracking up but me.

"That's really mean," I said, narrowing my eyes. "I hope if something embarrassing happens to any of you, nobody acts it out."

They all stopped laughing and stared at me.

"Oh come on, Heather. He had it coming. Stefan's a jerk," said one of the guys.

"No he's not!" My fists clenched at my sides.

"You clearly don't spend as much time around him as we do," said Jeffrey. "I'm surprised nobody's ever done worse than shove him. He calls our basketball team the Brick Throwers." He stood a little taller. "And I'm averaging thirty points per game!"

"And he calls any guy in choir girly," said someone else.

I turned to Emmett to see what his problem with Stefan was, but all he could do was sheepishly put his hands into his pockets. "You're right. It's not nice of us to make fun of him."

Jeffrey and the other guys booed and pushed him.

"Look, she's friends with Stefan." Emmett raised his voice to be heard above them. "And any friend of Heather's is a friend of mine." He nodded as if the argument was closed.

I couldn't help smiling. "Thank you," I said. "Now, what did you guys do this weekend?"

"Emmett saw *Fluffy Monkeys Go Bananas!*" one of the guys hooted, and as they teased him, he pointed at me.

See what you started? he mouthed.

I giggled and backed away, mouthing, *Sorry!*

After choir practice, there was still time before homeroom, so I pulled on my coat and ventured outside to catch up with Brooke and Vanessa. I knew Tim might be there too, but I would run into him in Journalism, anyway, so it was time to put the awkwardness aside.

Sure enough, the three of them were standing around the fountain talking, and when Tim looked over, I lost my breath for a second.

He wasn't scowling, but he wasn't smiling, either. His face was expressionless, as if I were a stranger.

I guess I deserved that.

Taking one deep breath, I approached my friends and waved.

Brooke and Vanessa waved back.

"Hey, look who it is," said V. "It's our friend Heather." She looked at Tim when she said this. "Isn't it nice to see our friend?"

Tim didn't react.

"Maybe this might help," I said, reaching into my gym bag. "I'm so sorry I didn't tell Stefan the truth about the eyeball. I'll tell him today. I promise." I pulled out another, smaller gift basket and presented it to Tim.

"Awww," said Brooke and Vanessa.

Tim looked at the contents. His lips quivered. His eyebrows wiggled. Then he burst out laughing.

Brooke, V, and I exchanged confused looks.

"What's so funny?" I finally asked.

Tim reached into the basket and pulled out what I'd bought him: a four-pack of Greek yogurt. He took a deep breath and laughed even harder, puffs of steam filling the air.

"I . . . I thought you liked that stuff. You schedule your day around it," I said with a frown. I looked to Brooke and Vanessa again.

"I do," he said with another snicker. "You just . . . don't even know."

I couldn't get the frown off my face. I was too confused. "Do you at least accept my apology?"

Tim took another deep breath, but this time he didn't laugh. Instead, he nodded.

"I do. Stefan was going to get me for laughing, anyway," he said. "But knowing you'll say something to him means a lot."

"Thanks for understanding," I said, giving him a hug.

Brooke snorted. "Please. He should be thanking you."

"Don't tell her that!" said Tim. "She'll take back the yogurt!" He clutched the basket to him.

"Why should he thank me?" I asked.

Vanessa glanced around and smiled. "Just wait a minute."

And in even *less* than a minute, two girls squealed and ran over.

"Tim! We heard about the fight!"

"Oh my God! Are you okay?"

One of them reached out and touched his cheek while the other hung on his arm.

"Does anything hurt?"

Tim smiled and preened.

I turned to Brooke and Vanessa. "Unbelievable."

"It's been like that all morning," said Brooke. "He's already had three different girls ask him to Fall Into Winter."

"What is he telling people?" I asked.

"The truth," said Vanessa. "That Stefan attacked him for something he didn't do."

"Oh, of course you didn't!" I heard one of

the girls say to Tim. "Everyone knows what a jerk Stefan Marshall is."

I was about to interject when Brooke grabbed my arm.

"Don't argue that point in front of him, behind him, or any place within hearing distance. They're mortal enemies now."

"That might be a tad dramatic, don't you think?" I asked.

Brooke let me go. "Suit yourself, but if you want Tim to believe you're really sorry about what happened, you won't defend Stefan."

It was easier said than done, though. Especially after I sneaked a peek at Stefan sitting in his homeroom. No girls were gushing over him, but they were giving him plenty of strange looks. The eighth grader who picked a fight with a sixth grader. And lost.

In my morning classes, I had to listen to everyone talk about the fight between Tim and

Stefan. Apparently, I was the only person in the entire school who didn't think he was a jerk. Now more than ever, he could definitely use a pick-me-up from a sweet, caring girl.

At lunch, the conversation started with Brooke telling Tim, "I'm glad he didn't hit you in the face. That could've affected your after-school . . . modeling career?" She stared closely at him.

Tim stared right back. "Huh?"

"Sorry, I meant your . . . movie role?" Brooke's eyes never left his.

Tim looked from me to Vanessa. "Did she get hit in the head with a soccer ball?"

"Oh, that damage was done a long time ago," said Vanessa.

"I think she's trying to figure out your secret double life," I said.

"That again?" asked Tim. "No, it's not modeling or movies. Although, you're right. I'd be perfect for both."

Vanessa and I snickered.

"If your work with the CIA didn't keep you busy?" asked Brooke, shifting in her seat to meet his eye again.

"Yes," said Tim. "I'm undercover, posing as an annoyed twelve-year-old."

"Geez, you'd think the CIA could afford better disguises," teased Vanessa.

The lunch bell rang, and we walked as a group to the newsroom, stopping to check the advice box, which held not only advice but notes to Tim.

> Way to go!
> Tim 1, Stefan 0.
> Will you fight someone for me?

"Well," Brooke said, handing him all the pieces of paper, "now you're getting attention from both the girls *and* guys."

187

"Nice," he said with a grin.

But his grin quickly vanished when we entered the room and Stefan approached him.

"Don't do anything stupid," Brooke told Tim, who was already clenching his fists.

"I won't," said Tim. "But I'm not going to let him come at me again."

Vanessa reached for my hand and I squeezed it to keep from throwing up.

Stefan didn't rush at Tim, though. Instead, he extended his hand.

"I'm sorry about what happened on Saturday. Truce?"

Tim nodded and shook it. "I'm sorry for laughing." He looked down at me and cleared his throat.

"Um . . . Stefan, can I talk to you over there for a second?" I nodded toward the pencil sharpener.

"Yeah, I owe you an apology too," he said.

"For the way I acted. And for wasting your pop-corn."

I smiled. "Oh, that's not a big deal. I'm sorry you feel so bad, though, and I thought of something that might cheer you up." I started turning him toward the bookshelf but stopped.

Someone had shoved a binder in front of the basket. All that I could see now was the handle.

Stefan nudged me. "What do you think would cheer me up? Because I could use it."

"Uhhh . . . a magic trick! But I need a pencil." I pointed to Mrs. H's desk. "Could you go get me one?"

Stefan gave me a strange look but nodded. "Okay, be right back."

While he made his way to the front of the classroom, I hurried over to the bookcase and pulled myself up the shelves, reaching for the basket-blocking binder. Once I had it, I leaped down and turned around, glancing at Mrs. H's desk to see if Stefan had seen me. He wasn't there.

There was a groaning sound behind me, and I looked over my shoulder, but there was nobody there . . . just the bookcase.

I squinted.

Which seemed to be getting closer.

And that's when I realized it was falling on me.

CHAPTER

10

Broken

"Look out!" someone shouted.

My feet were rooted to the spot. Only my arms seemed to be working, but they didn't feel like going any higher than chest level to cover my heart. I jammed my eyes shut and screamed.

And then the scream was knocked out of my throat as someone tackled me from the side, their arms locked tight around me. I stumbled sideways but managed to stay on my feet even as the bookcase fell beside me with a loud, floor-vibrating crash. I opened my eyes but couldn't see anything but a shirt pocket . . . Stefan's shirt pocket.

I could feel his heart beating a mile a minute, just like mine.

I was in heaven.

"Are you okay?" he asked, leaning away to check me over.

I nodded and croaked, "Thank you."

He stepped back a pace, and we looked around.

The wooden bookcase lay crookedly on top of some of the yearbooks that had dumped out as it tipped. All my classmates were staring at me and Stefan with wide eyes, and Mrs. H had her hand pressed to her heart while Mary Patrick had a hand over her mouth. Brooke, Vanessa, and Tim were all on their feet, as if they'd been planning to sprint the distance to get to me. And straight across from me, Gil was lowering his camera.

The perfect photo op.

"Are you okay?" Brooke screeched, running over with Vanessa and Tim right behind.

Everyone else seemed to break out of their trances as well, and the classroom was abuzz with conversation and movement as several students hurried over to help move books and broken pieces of shelf out of the way.

Stefan stepped back and maneuvered his way out of the debris. Instantly, he was surrounded by starstruck classmates, and I couldn't help feeling a little proud of myself as he smiled and talked with them.

It hadn't been my original plan, but Stefan's good mood had returned.

Brooke and Tim reached out to help me, but I waved them away.

"I'm fine. It completely missed me."

"That was lucky!" said Vanessa.

"Very," said Brooke, staring at the bookcase

with a frown. "What were you doing climbing on it, anyway?"

She was getting that Young Sherlocks look in her eye, but thankfully, Mrs. H bustled over with Mary Patrick and gripped my shoulders.

"Oh, I knew this was going to happen!" Mrs. H shook her head. "I should've had those cases bolted to the wall before the school year started. Are you hurt?" She had me turn a circle for her.

"I'm fine," I assured her. "Stefan saved me."

We looked over at him, now grinning and sitting on top of one of the desks, retelling the story of his daring rescue.

"I knew I only had seconds to save her," he said, "even if it meant putting my own life in peril."

Tim rolled his eyes. "Why did you *both* have to make it out okay?" he asked me.

I poked him. "Be nice. He called a truce, remember?"

Mrs. H clapped her hands. "Students, let's clear the rest of these books away so the custodial staff can haul off this death trap." She scowled at the bookcase as we all grabbed a stack of books and placed them against the wall. Shortly after, two men in jumpsuits appeared with a dolly and loaded up the busted furniture. I made sure I was right beside them so I could swoop in and throw my sweater over Stefan's gift basket, whisking it away.

When the chaos had died down and we were all back in our seats, Gil held out his camera and said, "What do you think?"

The image must have been taken seconds after the accident. It was of me and Stefan, my head tucked against his chest and his arms around me, books and bookcase scattered behind us.

We looked so good together, so comfortable and natural.

I drew in my breath. "It's perfect!"

This was another sign!

Forget about the invitation card. I was going to ask Stefan to Fall Into Winter in person.

Today.

Since it was Monday and newspapers were about to be distributed, Mrs. H had us go over "issues with the issue," little things that could be improved for future editions. After that, there wasn't much time left to break into our small groups, but when we did, I quickly confided my plan to my friends.

"Why?" asked Tim.

"Thank you for the vote of confidence," I said.

"Good luck!" said Vanessa, crossing her fingers. She elbowed Brooke, who nodded reluctantly.

"I hope you get what you want."

Getting through my next few classes was torture, but I used the time to rehearse exactly what I was going to say to Stefan. I waited until day's end when I knew he'd be alone and hung out in a classroom near his locker. As soon as I saw Stefan, I stepped out into the hall after him.

"Hey, Stefan!"

He turned and smiled. "Hey! Crazy day, huh?"

"You got that right!" I said, laughing like a hyena.

Maybe I should've stuck with the invitation card.

"I'm glad to see you're feeling better," I said. "You're definitely the hero of the day."

"Yep," he said, putting a book in his locker. "Positive attention is so much better than negative."

"I agree," I said, heart jackhammering against my chest. "In fact, you could probably get even *more* positive attention if you went to the Fall Into Winter dance with the girl you rescued."

He glanced back. "Huh?"

"I mean . . . do you want to go to the dance with me?" I blurted.

Stefan smiled and straightened, closing his locker. "Aw, that's sweet of you to worry about my popularity, but I think the rescue was enough of a ratings boost. Go have fun with one of your friends!"

He tousled my hair and walked away.

All I could do was stare after him.

What had just happened? Stefan thought I only wanted to go to the dance as a favor?

I had to correct it . . . now. While I had the courage.

Just as I was about to approach him, I saw Gil coming from the opposite direction. I ducked behind some lockers just as Stefan told Gil, "Well, I'm here. What do you need?"

"Just look at this photo one more time," said

Gil. "It's the perfect shot. I mean, right place, right time."

There was a beeping sound, like a digital camera.

"See right here?" said Gil. "There's a layer of dust coming up from the carpet where the bookcase landed."

I gripped the wall beside me. They were talking about the photo of Stefan and me!

"It would be a great shot," Stefan agreed, "if it was a different girl."

What? My heart dropped down to my feet. What did *that* mean?

"But Heather's really photogenic," said Gil.

I nodded in agreement.

"It's not that," said Stefan. "The photo . . . It's too . . . mushy. It looks like we're a couple."

My eyebrows furrowed. What was wrong with that?

And then Gil asked the question that was pounding in my head.

"What's wrong with that? You wouldn't go out with Heather?"

"Nope." I could practically see the disgust on Stefan's face, and my stomach tightened. "She's a cute kid, but Heather's like my little sister, dude. I would never go out with her."

In that moment, my heart shattered into a thousand pieces.

I leaned against the wall and choked back a sob.

There were no signs drawing us together. Following my heart had been stupid.

My face felt like it was on fire, and I couldn't stop swallowing at the lump in my throat, clenching and unclenching my fists and blinking back tears.

Heather's like my little sister. I would never go out with her.

My nose started to run. I could hear my heart beating in my ears. And then I heard Stefan mutter to himself.

"Shoot! I forgot my math book. Listen, man, I gotta get back to my locker."

"I'm still keeping it in case you change your mind," said Gil.

I didn't hear Stefan's response because I was already running fast and far. I rounded the corner into the sixth-grade hall and ducked into the girls' bathroom, locking myself in a stall and bursting into tears. My sobs and sniffles echoed off the walls, and I buried my face in my hands to quiet the sound.

After a minute or two, I had to stop crying because my nose was so stuffed I couldn't breathe. I sniffed hard and took a deep breath of air.

The bathroom door opened, and I stopped sniffling abruptly, peeking out of my stall.

When Brooke and Vanessa poked their heads around the edge of the door, my face crumpled and I held out my arms.

"Awww, sweetie!" Vanessa hurried toward me, squeezing me tight. "He said no?"

I shook my head as Brooke put her arms around both of us in a big bear hug. "He thought I was asking to be nice. But that isn't even the worst part!" I squeaked, my nose so stuffy it was hard to get the words out. "He was talking to Gil and . . ." I dissolved into tears again.

Brooke looked at Vanessa. "Go get Gil. Don't let Stefan see you."

V nodded, gave my hair a stroke, and ran out the bathroom door.

Brooke continued to hug me. "Are you going to be okay?"

I shook my head. "You were right, and I was dumb."

"You're *not* dumb." Brooke pulled away and

held my face in her hands. "You always follow your heart, and it is the best thing about you, and it's what makes you great with people. I wish I could be more like you." Her eyes teared up a little, and mine teared up even more.

"My heart led me off a cliff," I said with a sniffle.

Brooke laughed but quickly stifled it. "Sorry. But, Heather, he wasn't right for you. You can't see it now, but trust me. I've known you for seven years."

The bathroom door opened again, and V popped her head in. "Everyone decent?"

She walked in with Gil and Tim, both looking incredibly uncomfortable.

"Is this really a good idea?" asked Gil.

"We can't talk about this outside. People might hear," Vanessa told him.

"I've heard rumors about this place." Tim gazed around. "I didn't know it actually existed."

He touched my arm. "You okay?"

"I thought you had your . . . thing to go to," I said, sniffing hard again in an effort to get more air.

"I can be a little late," he said.

Brooke grabbed some paper towels and handed them to me.

"I forgot to tell Stefan the truth about the popcorn," I said, blowing my nose.

Tim chuckled. "It doesn't matter anymore. The girls think I'm a hero for that, the guys think he's a hero for rescuing you. . . ."

My lip quivered and Brooke pinched Tim. "Why'd you have to bring that up?"

Vanessa patted the counter. "Sit," she told me.

I hopped up and sat.

"Talk," she told me.

I repeated the story of how I'd asked Stefan to the dance, but he'd said no, so I'd chased after him. Then Gil repeated the conversation I'd overheard.

Even though I tried, I couldn't help crying again at how Stefan would never go out with me.

"But you asked him out!" said Vanessa, rubbing my arm. "That was really brave!"

"That guy's a jerk, anyway," said Brooke. "He's not good enough to date Heather. He's not good enough to date dirt!"

"Sorry," said Tim, giving me a side squeeze. "But what he thinks doesn't say anything about who you really are."

"Doesn't it?" I asked, balling up the paper towel in my hand. "I'm not good enough to date!" I slammed it into the trash.

"He never said that," Vanessa pointed out, tapping my leg. "He just said he didn't feel that way about you. It happens." She shrugged.

I sighed loudly. "I really wanted to go to the

dance with Stefan. I even asked him!"

"And you should be proud of yourself for that," said Brooke. "But it's not what he wanted. You have to move on. Trust me. You are meant to date someone sooo much better."

"No," I said, hopping down from the counter. "I'm never going to like anyone ever again. It's too painful."

My friends looked at one another.

"Man, I wish this was happening to one of you," said Tim, nodding to Vanessa and Brooke.

"Hey!" they both said.

"Well, Heather's the one who's good at relationship advice," he said. "She'd know exactly what to say if one of you were going through the same thing."

"Yeah, she would," said Brooke. She turned to me. "So how about it? What would you tell me if I was in your shoes and Stefan had said he'd never date me?"

"I'd say he's stupid," I immediately replied. "Because you're wonderful and amazing, and any boy would be lucky to be with you."

"And any boy would be lucky to be with *you*," Brooke told me. "You're wonderful and amazing, and if Stefan can't see that, he's stupid."

I couldn't help smiling. "You just repeated my words back to me."

"They're good words," said Brooke with a solemn nod. "What else?"

I thought for a moment. "Honestly? I'd probably give the advice all of you just gave to me. How he feels doesn't change your worth. You're just not his type, and you're meant for someone better." The pain inside me eased a bit, and I took a deep breath. "And that it takes a lot of courage to share your heart to begin with."

"Feeling okay now?" asked Vanessa with a smile.

"Not yet, but getting there." I wiped at my

eyes. "I just need some time. And to get my mind off it."

"No better place to do that than One Big Happy, where we get to watch all the kids play!" said Brooke. She checked her watch. "And we have to go!"

"I have to go too," said Tim. He gave me a hug. "Remember all the stuff that I told you at the movie theater. Stefan might not be right for you, but someone else is."

I nodded. "I know. Thanks."

"Can I leave too?" asked Gil, pointing to the door. "Please?"

"Sure," said Vanessa.

He waved to us and followed Tim out. Brooke caught the door and held up her phone.

"I'm going to call my mom and Mary Patrick and tell them we'll be a few minutes late," she told me and Vanessa. "Heather, are you okay?"

This time I nodded, and Brooke disappeared into the hall.

Vanessa studied my face. "Honey, I love you, but you are a mess. Time to get serious." She took some paper towels, wet them, and passed them to me. "Hold these on your face to reduce the swelling."

I did as she said, and while my eyes were covered, she brushed my hair and straightened my clothes. "Hold still. And close your eyes." She held up a white makeup pencil.

I backed away. "What are you going to do?"

"Hollywood trick," she said. "White on the inner corner of your eyelids makes you look more alert. It'll counteract the puffiness until your skin calms down."

"Is that one of the things you're doing for all your makeover clients?" I asked, clutching the counter with my fingertips. My clumsy friend with a pencil near my eye did not inspire confidence.

"If we have time," she said with a sigh. "We've got so many girls lined up that we'll barely have time to *breathe*."

"You should probably make an exception for that," I said with a smile. "But if you need help, I can be there. I mean, not to do makeup or anything, but to fetch supplies you might need or . . . I don't know . . . brush people's hair. That seems pretty simple."

"Really?" asked V.

I nodded. "Sure. It's not like I'm going to the dance with anyone," I added with a wry smile.

"Open your eyes," she said.

"Are we done already?" I asked.

"No, I just want you to see the delighted look on my face." Vanessa widened her eyes and grinned until all her teeth were showing.

"Yikes. Can I close my eyes again?"

She stuck her tongue out at me. "Despite that cruel comment, I will accept your offer of help."

Vanessa worked on my makeup for a few more minutes and instructed me to open my eyes again. I did so and looked in the mirror. Even though they were still sad, my eyes didn't look like I'd been bawling them out anymore. I hugged Vanessa.

"Thank you."

"It's the least I can do," she said, tickling me on the nose with a blush brush. "Come on. Let's go make some little kid's day."

We stepped out into the hall where Brooke was sitting against the wall and talking on her phone. When she heard us come out, she smiled and said into the phone, "Abel? I'll talk to you tonight. Bye!"

She got up and grabbed my hands. "Ready to rock it?"

I nodded. "Anything to get my mind off this afternoon."

We headed out to the van, where Brooke's mom was patiently waiting, and were on our way to the One Big Happy facility to meet the people we'd be working with.

Mary Patrick was waiting for us outside, foot tapping an angry rhythm on the pavement, and behind her, I saw a familiar figure snapping pictures of the building.

Stefan.

"Oh no," said Vanessa, Brooke, and I all at the same time.

He'd come to One Big Happy after all.

And I was going to have to face him.

CHAPTER

11

Eyes Wide Open

B rooke could already tell what I was thinking. "Okay, stay calm," she said in a low voice as we climbed out of the van. "He doesn't know that you know."

"Right," said Vanessa. "Pretend you didn't overhear him."

"I didn't overhear him," I repeated under my breath.

We walked toward Mary Patrick and Stefan.

"You never liked him," said Brooke.

"I never liked him," I repeated.

"You don't think he's cute," said V.

I paused. "Haven't you seen his chin dimple?"

Brooke pushed me forward. "Be cool! He's just some guy."

But then Stefan looked up from his camera and asked, "What took you guys so long?"

And all advice about being cool went out the window . . . for my best friends, at least.

"What's it to you, jerkface?" Brooke snapped.

"Yeah, maybe *you* should've taken a little longer to run a comb through that messy hair!" added Vanessa, hand on one hip.

Stefan and Mary Patrick stared at them, wide-eyed.

"Huh?" he asked.

"'Huh?'" Brooke and Vanessa imitated him, putting on their dopiest expressions. If I hadn't been so mortified, I would've laughed.

"What's wrong with them?" Mary Patrick asked me.

"They're just in bad moods." I ushered her toward the door. "Should we go inside?"

After she'd walked through, I grabbed Brooke and Vanessa by their arms, giving them pinches nobody else could see.

"Please stop!" I whispered.

A perky-looking blond woman with a pony-tail was waiting for us just inside.

"Hi! I'm Stacey, and welcome to One Big Happy. Speaking of happy, I'm happy to share a little something with you." She winked and reached into a tote bag on her shoulder, pulling out some rolled-up bundles that she tossed to each of us.

Vanessa unrolled hers first and held it up. "T-shirts! Cute!"

We all slipped ours on over our clothes, and Stacey beamed. "Now, our program is for high school students, so you won't be working with the little kids on your own, but you can shadow the high schoolers to get a better idea of what we do here."

"What *do* you do here?" I asked.

"One Big Happy is all about creating a positive environment for the younger generation. Our Little Buddies as we like to call them," she said, gesturing for us to follow. We walked down a corridor lined with framed pictures of high schoolers and little kids doing various activities together, all with great big smiles. "Most of our Little Buddies come from underserved families, so something as simple as a trip to the movies is great for them. But it's not all about having fun. We also teach."

She paused in front of a room with a wide bay window set into it. We peered inside at a high schooler standing by a chalkboard with a bunch of little kids gathered around her. She was drawing a head on a hangman as all the little kids groaned.

"It teaches them spelling," said Stacey.

"Do you charge kids to come to the program?" asked Mary Patrick.

She shook her head. "It's all funded through donations and fund-raisers," she said.

We kept walking past other windows with high schoolers working with more children.

"There are so many kids here," said Brooke. "They're all underserved?"

"Most," said Stacey. "Some of them are just kids who can't make it into regular after-school activities or weekend programs for various reasons."

She opened a door that led to a gymnasium, where a heated game of kickball was happening.

"Oh!" Brooke poked her head under Stacey's arm, and Stacey laughed.

"Care to join them?"

Brooke waved to the rest of us. "Later!"

Stefan lingered in the doorway to take a picture of Brooke charging across the floor to join the game, and when he lowered his camera, he smiled at me. "You're not going with her?"

My voice caught in my throat for a moment at how easily he could go from being disgusted at the thought of dating me to acting like nothing was wrong.

Of course to him, nothing *was* wrong.

"I'm not into sports," I said.

"Really?" He cocked his head to one side and smiled. "Oh, you're more the drama club type, huh?"

"No," I said in a slightly offended tone. Did he really know that little about me? I could fill a notebook with the things I knew about him. Heck, I literally had! "I'm in choir."

"Ohh," he said. "Yeah, you should be. You've got a nice voice."

"Thanks," I said, but for some reason, it didn't thrill me to get a compliment from him the way it used to.

"Heather?" Vanessa called to me from the bottom of a short flight of stairs. "Are you guys coming?"

"Yep!" I hurried down the stairs and hooked my arm through hers while Stacey told Mary Patrick about the amount of money it took just to keep the facility running.

"Some years it's harder than others," she admitted. "And the equipment gets a little run-down before we can afford new stuff. But we always get by."

"So since kids our age can't watch the Little Buddies, how can we help?" I asked.

"We always take donations and help for

our fund-raisers," she said. "You might not be old enough to mentor our Little Buddies, but you can run the snack table at one of our movie nights, for instance. Speaking of which . . ." Stacey placed her hand on a door. "Through here is our cafeteria. I think you guys are lucky enough to be here for snack time *and* a movie."

She held the door wide open, and the most wonderful heavenly smell wafted out.

"Popcorn!" I said with a happy sigh.

"Are you a fan?" asked Stacey, regarding me with an amused smile.

"She will probably trample you to get to it," Vanessa warned her.

Stacey held up her hands in mock fright and stepped back so I could pass.

There was a pleasant, smiling woman in a white apron handing out bags to the kids. When she saw us approach, she smiled even bigger.

"Our Little Buddies are growing!" she

commented, holding out a bag to Stefan.

He flinched and turned away. "I'm gonna pass."

"What's the matter?" Vanessa asked with a smirk. "Had your fill of eyeballs?"

I pressed my lips together to hide a smile.

Stefan scowled at her. "You would've done the exact same thing in my shoes."

"No." Vanessa glanced down at his feet and curled her lips. "I would not be caught dead in shoes like that."

I bumped her. "V, be nice," I said. Then I thanked the smiling woman as she passed me a bag of popcorn.

Stefan snapped a few pictures of the kids hanging out in the cafeteria, watching an animated movie projected on the wall.

"Do you have any Reese's cups?" Mary Patrick asked the woman in the apron.

She shook her head.

"Snickers? Twix? Any chocolate?" Mary Patrick kept trying, wringing her hands together anxiously. "It's been almost two hours since I've had any chocolate!"

"This isn't a concession stand," Vanessa told her.

Finally, Mary Patrick accepted the popcorn and sighed.

Stacey smiled and leaned close to her. "We do have vending machines in the corner."

Instantly, Mary Patrick thrust her popcorn at me and started fishing through her purse for change.

Stacey held her arms wide. "Well, you've seen the whole facility, so feel free to roam around and watch us in action. And if you see any Little Buddies by themselves, let one of us know, won't you?"

We thanked her for her time, and she left the group. In a moment, Mary Patrick did the same, hurrying off to the vending machine. That left me and Vanessa standing with Stefan.

I wasn't sure if Vanessa had any more unexpressed Stefan rage to let out, but I didn't want to wait and find out.

"Come on." I nudged her. "Let's go mingle with the little kids."

We made our way to a crowded table that had popcorn strewn across it. Tiny hands reached into the pile, stuffing tiny mouths. I added Mary Patrick's bag to the mix and sat beside a girl wearing a polka-dot dress and fairy wings.

She gazed up at me with curious eyes.

"Who are you?" she asked.

"I'm Heather."

"Are you a Big Buddy?" She tilted her head. "You don't look so big."

"No," I said, crouching. "I'm little!"

The girl laughed. "No you're not!"

"I'm not?" I wrinkled my forehead. "Then what am I?"

"You're a princess!"

I smiled. "And what are you?"

"I'm your fairy godmother." She took out a handful of popcorn and threw it at me. "Ta-da!"

I acted as if she'd magically transformed me. "Oh my goodness!"

She turned to Vanessa and did the same thing. Vanessa struck a diva pose, and the girl giggled again.

"That's not how princesses act!"

Vanessa put her hands on her hips. "And how would you know, Fairy Godmother?"

The girl didn't have an answer for that. Instead, she turned to look up at someone behind me. "Who are you?" I turned and realized Stefan had followed us over to the table.

"I'm a photographer," he said, holding up his camera.

"I'm a photographer too!" she said. "Wanna see?" Without waiting for an answer, she scurried away and returned a moment later with a plastic toy camera.

Stefan chuckled. "That's not a camera; that's a toy."

She looked at it. "No, it's not."

"Yes, it is," he said, taking it from her. "See? The buttons don't even work."

Her lower lip trembled.

"Stefan, give her back the camera," I said in a low voice.

He held it out, and she swiped it with an injured look. "The buttons do too work," she said. "You're not pressing them right." She held the plastic camera to her eye and made a clicking sound with her tongue. "See?"

"You didn't really take my picture," he said with an arrogant smirk.

"I did so!" she said in a voice that was dangerously close to a shriek.

"Then show it to me," he said.

Vanessa and I glanced at each other.

"Stefan, why are you arguing with a five-year-old?" I asked.

"Because she's being ridiculous," he said.

"She's being five!" said Vanessa. She tugged on the little girl's hand. "Hey, would you take my picture?"

The little girl's expression turned serious and she nodded, holding the camera to her eye.

Vanessa smiled wide and cheesy for the camera, and the girl made a clicking noise.

"Thank you!" said Vanessa, and the little girl beamed and swayed back and forth shyly. V looked up at Stefan as if to say, *See?*

"Whatever," he scoffed. "I'm going to get a soda."

We watched him leave as Mary Patrick walked toward us, then turned her head in Stefan's direction and made a strange face before approaching the table where Vanessa and I were sitting.

"Hey, Heather, can I talk to you for a second?" she asked.

I exchanged a mystified look with Vanessa, but got to my feet. "Sure."

Mary Patrick pulled me away from the table and tore open a package of Reese's peanut butter cups. "Listen, I know it's none of my business," she said, liberating the chocolate from its wrapper. "But Stefan is trouble. Trust me, I know firsthand." She shoved the entire peanut butter cup into her mouth.

I stared at her, wide-eyed, and she swallowed hard. "Sorry, I'd offer to share, but . . . I don't want to."

I waved a dismissive hand. "That's not why I'm staring. *You* dated Stefan?"

Mary Patrick looked insulted. "You say that

like it's impossible. He's not a rock star."

"Of course not," I said. "Sorry. He just doesn't seem like your type."

She smirked. "You figured that out faster than I did. He's a nice enough person." She took her time peeling the paper wrapper off the second Reese's. "And if you don't mind me saying, he's not your type, either." She glanced up. "I know I don't know you that well, but I know *him* that well. So just . . . be careful."

"You don't have to worry," I assured her. "I don't like him."

The strange thing was . . . I really meant it.

Stefan had never bothered to get to know me. He was rude to my friends. He crushed little girls' dreams, *and* he'd refused free popcorn. Who did that?

"Really?" asked Mary Patrick. "Because I thought—"

I shook my head. "Nope. There's nothing there."

Instantly, I felt more at ease and lighter than I had in a long time.

"Hey, what's going on?" Stefan asked, walking up to me and Mary Patrick.

He took a giant swig of soda and, curling his lip, let out a tremendous belch. Everyone at the table stared at him, and he grinned.

"Impressed? There's more where that came from," he promised.

I gave Mary Patrick a nauseated look. "Definitely nothing," I said.

And then we both started to laugh.

CHAPTER

12

Happier Ever After

When I got home later that afternoon, Bubbe and Mom were in the kitchen, drinking tea and going over the Thanksgiving menu.

"Hey, sweetheart. How was One Big Happy?" Mom held open her arms and I walked into them for a hug.

"Fun," I said. "The kids were really sweet and . . . What, Bubbe?"

She was regarding me with a shrewd expression.

"Something's different," she said, pointing at

my face. "You look happier." She gasped. "Did you ask that boy to the dance?"

Mom held me at arm's length. "What boy? There's a boy?"

"Oops." Bubbe pressed the tips of her fingers to her lips.

"No, there's no boy," I said. "That's why I'm happier."

Mom shook her head. "I'm lost."

"There *was* a boy," I said. "But he didn't turn out to be worthy of me." I jutted my chin out, and Bubbe hooted with laughter.

"Good for you!"

Mom smiled. "Is this what Tim and you were disagreeing about?"

I nodded. "He was right. And we made up."

"Good," said Mom, passing me some menu cards. "Now, help us pick a dessert."

"Apple pie," I said without even looking down.

"You don't want to know more about the boy?"

Mom shrugged. "What's to know? He wasn't good enough for my daughter, he isn't worth mentioning." She leaned forward and kissed me on the forehead. "We already have apple pie on the menu. Pick something else."

So I sat at the table with them and talked about Thanksgiving and my volunteer work and the Model UN and the newspaper . . . Everything but boys, which was fine with me.

When they started cooking dinner, I headed to my room to do some catching up on the advice column. But before that, I had to do a little decluttering. Vanessa's magazines were all over the floor, pages folded down where there were boy-catching articles. And my desk was overflowing with gift ideas, "Penny Wishes" song lyrics, and the advice request to Heartbroken in Homeroom that I'd been meaning to answer. Now, I had my own insight to go off of.

I scooped up all the magazines and threw

them in the trash, along with anything on which I'd written Stefan's name, including my notebook. Then I got to work answering the question.

While I was in the middle of it, there was a knock on my door, which immediately opened.

"Mom says it's time for dinner," said Isaac.

I spun in my desk chair. "Hey, why did you go see *Stealing Ever After*?"

Instantly, he broke into a grin. "Can't tell you."

I rolled my eyes. "Is it some dumb boy thing?" When he didn't answer, my eyes widened. "It is! What is it?"

"Berryville Sporting Goods is holding a contest," he said. "It's like a scavenger hunt, and one of the items you have to turn in is a picture of yourself with Sleeping Beauty's prince behind you."

"Prince Philip?" I asked.

"Sure," said Isaac with a shrug. "If that's who Adrenaline Dennis plays."

"Who?" I asked with a furrowed brow.

"Adrenaline Dennis," he repeated. "You know, the famous motocross racer?"

I shook my head. "No clue. So that's why you saw it?"

My brother pulled his phone out of his back pocket and showed me the photo. Sure enough, he was sitting sideways in a theater seat, pointing at Prince Philip on the screen beside him.

"The prize is five hundred dollars' worth of free sports apparel from Berryville Sporting Goods."

"Huh." I leaned back. "Do they sell swimming and surfing equipment?"

"They sell everything," he said.

"That explains a lot." At Isaac's inquisitive look, I added, "Some guys at my school were talking about it. Did you actually like it?"

He scratched his head. "I only stayed long enough to take the photo."

"But that scene is in the beginning of the movie!" I pointed at his phone. "You wasted money just for the photo?"

"Kids?" Dad called from downstairs. "We don't want the food to get cold."

"It wasn't a big deal," Isaac told me.

"For some people, getting to go to the movies is a *huge* deal," I said, thinking about what Stacey had said at One Big Happy.

"Kids!" Dad's voice was getting louder. "Don't make me use my powers of Dad-itude."

"You only have power over numbers!" Isaac shouted back, grinning.

I jumped up and grabbed his arm. "Isaac!"

He recoiled, startled. "What——?"

"You're brilliant!" My dad *did* have powers, and I was going to ask him to use them. "Come on, let's go!"

"All right," said Isaac, following me downstairs, "but I'm going to start charging you for these great ideas I come up with but know nothing about."

"I'll make it up to you with some popcorn if you see *Stealing Ever After* with me," I offered.

Isaac made a face. "That's a chick flick. Besides, I thought you had some dance this weekend."

I waved the idea away. "I'm not going."

"Oh. Too bad." He shrugged and dropped the subject.

But when I gave my friends the same answer the next day at lunch, they weren't as quick to let it go.

"What do you mean you're not going?" asked Brooke. "Vanessa and I can't go without you! Nobody's ever heard of the Two Musketeers."

"In case you haven't noticed, I don't have a date," I pointed out.

"You know if you asked Emmett, he'd go with you," said Tim. "Don't you like him?"

"I don't know," I said, picking apart my hamburger. "It would feel like I'm asking him just to have someone to go with, and I don't want to do that. I'd rather just see what happens."

"You mean you haven't started a stalker journal about him yet?" asked Brooke.

I threw a fry at her.

"Thank you!" she said, popping it in her mouth.

"No more journals for me," I said. "No more daydreams about guys, no more writing their name on my palm so I can carry them around with me all day . . ."

Tim raised his eyebrow. "You do that?"

I froze. "No."

Brooke sighed and speared a forkful of salad. "What will Stefan do without you?"

"I'm sure he'll find another girl to swoon over

him. Besides, I'm going to be too tired to dance after helping V!"

Vanessa held up a hand, and I high-fived it.

"So you're just going to go to bed early?" asked Brooke.

"Of course not. I'll go see *Stealing Ever After* again. And I'll let you in on a secret," I said. I leaned forward and waited until they were all listening. "If you guys want to go, you can get in for the cost . . . of two canned goods. All night." I sat back and waited for their reactions.

"What?" asked Brooke, wide-eyed. "I can pay for my movie with tuna?"

"Seriously?" squeaked Vanessa, knocking over her soda.

"How do you know this?" Tim asked me with a dubious expression.

"I had my dad set it up with Martin Hess this morning," I said with a proud smile. "You know the guy who owns the theater? Since he's already going to lose business because of the dance, my dad convinced him to draw people to the theater by offering free showings of *Stealing Ever After* and *Fluffy Monkeys Go Bananas* for food donations. That way, he still gets a crowd and money from concessions, and the food bank gets even more supplies!"

"That's awesome!" said Brooke. Then she frowned. "But why *Fluffy Monkeys Go Bananas?*"

"So Stefan will have something to watch that's more his speed," said Tim.

"Be nice," I said, wagging a finger at him. "No, I asked my dad to include *Fluffy Monkeys Go Bananas* so the kids at One Big Happy would have something to watch."

"Ohhh," my friends chorused.

"As soon as my dad gave me the okay this morning, I called Stacey and told her," I continued. "She said they'd let all the parents know to bring in cans, and One Big Happy would pick up the tickets."

V's forehead wrinkled. "But what about the kids who can't even afford to bring in cans?"

My triumphant smile wavered. "Oh. I hadn't thought of that."

Tim snapped his fingers. "Let me talk to my folks. I'm sure they can spare some stock at one of the stores."

Tim's parents owned a few corner markets.

"That would be great!" I reached out to high-five him. "And we can put up a flyer in Locker 411, so everyone knows about it."

Brooke clapped her hands. "Good job, Heather!" She paused and winced. "But I'm still going to the dance."

"Yeah, me too," said Vanessa, grabbing my hands. "Sorry!"

I smiled and nodded. "Not a problem. What about you?" I bumped Tim with my elbow. "You want to come to the movies?"

Tim gave me an arrogant smile. "Heather. Sweetie. You don't think old Timmy's got a date for the dance?"

"Do you?" asked Vanessa.

He tilted his hand from side to side. "I'm still narrowing down the list."

"Narrowing down the list," said Brooke with a snort. "How many girls asked you?"

"Probably none. He's going with Gabby," teased Vanessa.

Brooke smacked her palm on the table. "That's the big secret! You're going to the dance with your sister!"

"Shhh! No, it's not!" said Tim, making a keep-it-down motion with his hand.

"Then what is your big secret?" asked Brooke. "I've used all my Young Sherlocks skills to find out. I asked your sister, I asked your mail carrier—"

"My mail carrier?"

"I even tailed you once to see where you were going."

Both of Tim's eyebrows went up.

"And you guys thought *I* was weird for having a Stefan journal," I said.

Brooke pointed at me. "No, that's still incredibly weird. And I'm not weird; I'm focused."

"Fine," said Tim. "You want to know what I've been up to?"

"Yes!" said Brooke, collapsing her upper body onto the table.

"You really need to hear about it?"

"Yes," I said.

"You have to find out my big secret?"

"Is it that you're deaf?" asked Vanessa. "Because you don't seem to be hearing us. YESSSS!" she said, nodding in an exaggerated fashion.

Tim took a deep breath and let it out. "You

promise you won't laugh?"

"Yes," said me and Vanessa.

Brooke stayed silent, and we all looked at her.

"I can't make a promise like that," she said with a shrug. "If he's a professional kitten groomer, I will laugh." She paused. "And then I'll ask if he can fit Chelsea in on Thursday."

Vanessa, Tim, and I laughed.

"Well, I'm sorry to let you down, but I'm not a kitten groomer," said Tim.

He leaned close.

So did we.

"As you know, my family is Greek."

Brooke gasped and clutched V's arm. "He's a prince!"

"Shush, or he's not going to tell us!" I hissed. Then I gestured to Tim. "Continue."

"My family is Greek," he repeated, "and they're very big on tradition." He reached for his phone and flipped through some photos. "So my big secret . . . is that I'm a Greek folk dancer."

He turned his phone so we could see a photo.

There was Tim, wearing a white blouse under an embroidered vest, a fluffy white skirt, white stockings, and loafers with massive pompoms on the toes.

I clapped a hand over my mouth and fought back a laugh. Vanessa pressed her lips together and made a sound like a boiling teakettle. Brooke didn't even try to hold back. She let loose a guffaw and slapped the table.

"I'm so glad I decided to share this with you," said Tim, pocketing his phone with a frown. "Really. This is a safe space."

"I'm so sorry!" said Brooke, putting a hand on his arm that slowly slid off as she fell out of her chair, giggling.

Poor Tim looked so hurt that I pinched myself to regain my composure.

"We're sorry," I said. "We should be more

supportive of you and your culture." I gave Vanessa a meaningful look and stepped on Brooke's hand.

"Owww," she said through her laughter. "We're sorry."

"So the . . . dancing is what you've been busy doing?" I asked.

Tim nodded. "Our whole dance troupe is going to be performing at the Museum of Science and Industry at Christmastime, so we've been practicing extra hard."

"Aww, that's great!" I said.

"No, it's not," he said, slumping his shoulders. "Because if you guys laughed and you're my friends, imagine what everyone else in school is going to do when they find out."

"No way!" Instantly, Brooke was back in her seat. "Anyone makes fun of you, and they'll have *us* to deal with." She put her fist on the center of the table. "Right, guys?"

"Right!" said Vanessa, covering Brooke's hand with her own.

"Right!" I said, placing mine on both of theirs.

Tim smiled. "Thanks, guys."

"Well, come on." Brook nodded toward our hands. "You have to join us."

He sighed. "This isn't going to help my image." He placed his hand on ours. "What are we cheering?"

We all thought for a moment.

"What's a Greek saying?" asked Brooke.

"*Opa?*" suggested Tim.

"Let's do it," said Vanessa.

Brooke counted to three, and we lifted our hands into the air. "*Opa!*"

The lunch bell rang, and we gathered our stuff to head to Journalism.

"I have a feeling Mary Patrick's going to ask about our article today. Overall, how did you guys feel about volunteering?" I asked.

"Something I can put in the piece."

We sat down in our corner of the room, and Brooke said, "It makes me more appreciative of what I have when I see what others don't have."

"I like that," I said, smiling as I wrote. "Tim?"

"It helped me realize how much money we waste every day without even knowing it. You could buy a basketball that kids could play with all year for the cost of a pizza you'd eat in one evening."

"What about you, V?" I asked, jotting down Tim's comment.

"I learned that it's easy for anyone to help out," she said. "And it makes you feel really good to do it."

"What about you?" Brooke asked me. "What did you learn?"

I thought for a moment. "That there are some really great people out there. And I'm talking to three of them."

"Awww." Vanessa leaned over and hugged me. "Don't forget to look in the mirror for the fourth."

Mrs. H called the class to attention, and we provided our progress updates. The front page mentioned a new piece they were working on . . . how sportswriter-photographer Stefan Marshall had saved fellow columnist Heather Schwartz from certain death by falling bookcase.

"Oh brother," I muttered.

Once again Gil and Stefan argued about using the photo he'd taken, but this time . . . it was reversed.

"That was a really good photo," said Stefan.

"I don't think we should use it," said Gil, no doubt thinking of me. "Besides, yesterday weren't you saying—"

"It's proof that it happened!" Stefan blurted.

"Aaand the truth finally comes out," said Tim

in a low voice. "He wants to use that image to repair *his* image."

"Heather." Stefan glanced back at me. "Don't you think they should run the picture?"

I shook my head. "It'll take up too much space. Then we won't be able to run one of the pictures you took from the volunteering gigs. Wouldn't it be nice to have an article about you *and* a photo credit?"

He chewed his thumbnail. "Good point."

The news team went back to talking, and my friends gave me a strange look.

"Don't tell me you're sweet on him again," said Vanessa.

"I'm not," I said. "He's right. It looks too couply, and I don't want anyone else to see that picture."

My friends exchanged sly glances.

"Anyone . . . in particular?" asked Tim.

"Maybe," I said with a secretive grin. "You want to hear the advice I posted on the website for Heatbroken in Homeroom?"

"Bring it on," said Brooke.

So I read what I'd put together, and when I was finished, my friends gave me a standing ovation.

"Are my ears playing tricks on me?" asked Tim. "Or did I hear some of my advice in there?"

"Once in a while you get lucky and say something smart," I told him with a wink.

"You should have listened to me from the beginning, you know," he said.

"But if I had, I wouldn't have learned 'Penny Wishes' to impress you-know-who, and I wouldn't have decided to sing it in solo tryouts tomorrow."

It took a minute for what I'd said to sink in, but when it did, both Brooke and Vanessa screamed and jumped up and down. Everyone else in the newsroom looked at us as if we'd gone crazy. So did Tim. In fact, he might have shrunk down in his seat a little.

I giggled and shushed my friends. "I haven't gotten the solo yet."

"But you will!" cried Vanessa, wrapping her arms around me and rocking from side to side.

"You're going for a solo!" screeched Brooke. "We're so proud of you!"

"Well, thank you for the votes of confidence," I said.

"Advice team!" Mary Patrick's voice sounded sharply across the room. "I can't hear myself think!"

"Sorry," Brooke, Vanessa, and I chorused.

In a quieter voice, Brooke said, "Heather, if you need *anything* to prep, let us know."

"Yeah, if you need us to show up and be your cheerleaders, we're there," agreed V.

Tim cleared his throat. "I'll be there to show

support, but I won't be a cheerleader."

"Why not?" asked Brooke with a wide grin. "You already have the skirt."

"Ohhh!" said Vanessa.

"I'm never telling you anything again," said Tim.

"Awww," I said, giving him a shoulder squeeze. "You know we're behind you no matter what."

"And I'm behind you," he said, extending his fist. "Good luck tomorrow."

I bumped it with my own. "Thanks," I said. "But I need courage more than anything."

"You'll find it," he said. "Just dig deep. If you could do it for Stefan, you can do it for yourself."

And he was right.

The next morning, I walked to the front of the choir room, heart pounding, palms sweating, all eyes and ears on me. I took one deep breath and sang "Penny Wishes" from the depths of my soul.

Honestly, I was still a little nervous, so I kept my eyes closed for most of the song, but whenever I opened them, I just saw smiles and pleased faces. In fact, there were even a few tears.

The last word left my lips, and there was a moment of silence, followed by whistling and applause.

"Why haven't you auditioned for me sooner?" asked Miss Thompson, giving me a hug.

At the end of it all, Emmett came up to me and bowed.

"What's that for?" I asked with a giggle.

"I'm humbled by your greatness," he said. "And I want to be the first to congratulate you on your solo."

I shyly clasped my hands behind my back and studied the carpet. "Well, I don't have it *yet*."

"You will," he said with confidence.

"Thanks," I said, picking up my book bag.

He walked with me to the door and opened it.

"Word in the halls is that you're skipping the Fall Into Winter dance," he said.

"Yeah, I'm not much of a dancer," I lied. "Plus, there's this really good movie out I want to see."

"Oh yeah? What is it?"

I grinned. "*Stealing Ever After*."

"What?" Emmett laughed. "What is this, your third time to see it?"

"Second and a half," I argued. "I didn't get to see all of it last time."

"Oh right," he said with a nod. "Because of . . ." He waved his arms wildly and squinted one eye.

I giggled. "Something like that." I fiddled with the strap on my bag. "So are you going to the dance?"

"Nope," he said. "Someone asked me but I turned them down."

"Really? Why?"

Emmett shoved his hands into his pockets. "There's this movie I've been wanting to see:

Stealing Ever After. Have you heard of it?"

I pretended to think. "Hmmm."

"This cute girl in choir recommended it," he said.

I almost tripped over an invisible hump in the carpet, but Emmett caught my arm.

"She . . . she did?" I whispered.

He grinned. "Yep." The first bell sounded, and he pointed toward the ceiling. "Well, I should get to homeroom. See ya!"

I cleared my throat and called after him, "Seven o'clock!"

He turned around, and I clasped my hands in front of me. "Seven o'clock. That's the best showing to go to on Saturday. And this weekend, if you bring two canned goods, you get in free."

Emmett turned a little pink. "Maybe I'll see you there. We could protest the dance as a team. And I could get rid of some of the lima beans my mom always buys."

I smiled. Even though I wasn't quite ready to date again, maybe I didn't have to write it off entirely.

"I'll save you a seat," I told Emmett. Then I hummed "Penny Wishes" all the way down the hall.

Dear Heartbroken in Homeroom,

Congratulations on putting your heart out there! Sometimes we're scared of what a crush might think of us, so we don't even try, but it's better to know than to wonder "What if?"

First, ask yourself why you like the guy. Do you have a lot in common? Does he treat you nicely? Does he treat other people nicely? If you answered yes to all of the above, then put on your most confident smile and start with "Hi." If he responds positively, pay him a genuine compliment or ask his opinion on something. Make a personal connection and let

things unfold from there. If it ever feels forced
or like too much work, then let it go. A good
relationship comes naturally.

Oh, and make sure he likes your favorite
food . . . but not so much that he eats it all.

Confidentially yours,

Heather Schwartz

Acknowledgments

Always for my family, friends, and God.

For my big sister, Cindy, who always brags on me and laughs so easily. I will come to Japan, I promise!

For the Austin writing community, who are always there with the assist.

For Laurie Hill Roberts, who helped me create my beloved sanctuary.

And for Kami, Lisa, and Mandy, who are *my* Three Musketeers.

Turn the page for a sneak peek at the next book
in the Confidentially Yours series:

CHAPTER

1

Greek Out

I should've been named Apollo.

I know it's pretty bold comparing myself to the Greek god of light, but Mr. Sunshine and I have a lot in common: We're both Greek, we both have twin sisters, we're both into culture, and we both value honesty more than . . .

Okay, that last one's a stretch. For me, the truth's a gray area, and whether I tell it depends on how much I'll suffer.

For example, if a girl asks, "Does this shirt look stupid?," I'm never going to tell the truth. Ever.

Because I did once.

Getting hit with a bag hurts a lot more than you'd think.

Anyway, apart from the fact that Apollo was a god and I'm mortal, we're practically the same guy.

"Practically," I said to the crumbling marble statue in front of me. Poor Apollo was missing an arm, half his face, and a leg. "Although, you seem a little more accident-prone."

"There is *no* way you saw me smack into that display case," said a voice beside me. "I was all the way across the room!"

I grinned and turned to my friend Vanessa Jackson, who was cradling one hand. Our history class was on a field trip to the Berryville art museum, and we were all given specific instructions not to touch *anything*.

Those words have no meaning to a group of twelve-year-olds.

"I wasn't talking to you," I said. "But let me guess. You tried to reach through the glass?"

Poor V tends to be a little on the clumsy side.

"It's just so clear!" she said, massaging her fingers. Then she looked up at Apollo. "I'm guessing you were talking to this guy. That's cool. Sometimes I talk to my dummy."

I gasped in mock horror. "What a mean thing to call your brother!"

Vanessa giggled and punched my arm with her good hand. "No! My dressmaker's dummy."

V designs and makes her own clothes. I'm no fashion expert, but from what I've seen, she seems to know her stuff. There's never an extra neck hole or anything.

Her style savvy is probably why her answers for the advice column are so popular. Vanessa and I, along with our friends Heather Schwartz and Brooke Jacobs, answer cries for help in "Lincoln's Letters," the advice column for Abraham

Lincoln Middle School's newspaper, the *Lincoln Log*.

V dishes fashion advice, Heather gives friendship and relationship advice, and Brooke tackles health and fitness. I, Tim Antonides, round it out by providing the male perspective on issues, but to be honest, sometimes I wish I did health and fitness instead. Sports are a huge part of my life, and there's never a season when I'm not in some sort of uniform. Brooke is a sports nut too, but she can't give the guy's point of view like I can.

For now, I settle with being the secondary sportswriter. The stories I'm assigned aren't that interesting ("Football Team Gets New Footballs!"), but I'm working really hard to impress so that someday I can be bumped up to head sportswriter.

"You talk to your dressmaker's dummy?" I asked V. "It doesn't even have a head."

"Oh, because if it did, there'd be a better

chance of me getting an answer?" she asked, laughing again.

For Vanessa, everything is a reason to laugh. She's one of the most upbeat people I know.

"Yeah, okay," I said. Then I pointed to Apollo. "Did you know that Apollo could see the future?"

"Neat. Did he see you getting left behind because everyone else is in the next room?" Vanessa asked, pointing toward an archway.

I glanced around. Other than Vanessa, not a single other person from class was with us.

"Oops," I said. "Let's go."

We jogged out of the room to catch up with our classmates, who were checking out an exhibit on Polynesia.

"... live in Hawaii today," our history teacher, Mr. Edwards, finished. He nodded to me. "Good of you to finally leave Greece and join us, Mr. Antonides."

I gave him an apologetic shrug. "My chariot had a flat."

I'm usually running late to stuff, so it's handy to keep a pocketful of excuses.

Mr. E smiled and gestured to another exhibit. "Dance is a large part of Polynesian culture. It is a way for them to tell stories, give thanks to the gods, and celebrate life in general."

"Ha! Check it out." A guy in our class pointed to a screen showing a video of a Polynesian dance.

I wouldn't say the advice column has any real enemies, but if we did, this kid Ryan Chapman would be the closest thing. When our very first issue came out, he argued that Brooke, a girl, shouldn't give sports advice. Then he went on to try to take her job at the newspaper, saying he could do better, which ended in an advice-off. *And* every time he catches me reading a book, he makes fun of the title, like referring to *The Wind in the Willows* as *The Wind from my Butt.*

So yeah, I'm not a Ryan fan.

The entire class gathered to watch the video of the Polynesian men who were hooting and hopping around.

"All the guys are wearing skirts," Ryan said with a laugh. "They look dorky."

"Hey!" cried Vanessa at the same time I said, "That's not dorky!"

Everyone's attention shifted from the video to V and me.

"I just started dating a guy from Hawaii . . . Gil Pendleton," explained Vanessa. "And if he wore a grass skirt, I wouldn't care." She frowned. "Unless he matched it with the wrong shirt."

Several people laughed.

"What about you?" A guy next to me, Berkeley Dennis, bumped my arm. "You seem almost as mad as Vanessa."

"Me?" I repeated.

Okay, so here's the thing.

I'm a Greek folk dancer. Sometimes our costumes have skirts. And tights. And shoes with fluffy pompoms on the toes. It doesn't look very cool, especially for the dance numbers when the guys hold hands and skip in a circle. Only five people at school know my secret, one of them being my sister, Gabby, but only because she dances too.

But nobody else is ever going to find out.

Especially not Berkeley Dennis.

Think of the coolest, sportiest, dudeliest guy you know. Now have him sitting on a pile of money. That's Berkeley.

I mentioned earlier that our advice column was pretty popular, and it gets me a lot of attention from the girls. Needless to say, a lot of guys don't like that. Ordinarily, I wouldn't care, but my best friend, Gus McDade, moved away over the summer, so I've been searching for new people to hang out with. Berkeley and I have a few classes together, and he helped rescue my shorts from the swimming pool when someone threw them in (seriously, the guys are *jealous*), so he's at the top of my potential friend list. But I had a feeling he wouldn't be if he knew of my frolicking ways.

As soon as Berkeley asked about my outburst, Ryan chimed in.

"Yeah, why does it bother you so much?" he asked with a smirk. "Do you dance around in a skirt too?"

The other kids snickered.

Nope. Nobody else was *ever* going to find out.

"Actually, I agree with Vanessa," I said in my calmest, coolest voice. "It's important to respect people's backgrounds. Just like I'd never insult *your* family for swinging from trees and scratching their armpits."

Everyone in the class roared with laughter. Except Ryan.

"Oh yeah?" he said. "Well, *your* family . . . They're . . ."

"Capable of complete sentences?" I finished for him. "Don't worry, Ape Man, you'll get there someday."

More laughter until Mr. E quieted everyone down. "Why don't we move on to Polynesian art?"

We all followed him into the next room, and Berkeley bumped my arm again. "Way to put him in his place."

"He's had it coming," I said. "Believe me."

He nodded. "Listen, my cousin Alistair's coming to town the weekend before Christmas, and a bunch of guys will be at my house to meet him. You should come."

I froze in my tracks, causing Vanessa to walk into me from behind.

"Sorry!" she said.

I didn't respond to her. I was too busy staring openmouthed at Berkeley.

"Alistair, as in Alistair Dennis? Your cousin is Alistair 'Adrenaline' Dennis?" I finally managed.

Berkeley grinned. "Well, to me, he's just Alistair, but yeah."

"Who's that?" asked V.

"Who's . . ." I regarded her with an expression of disbelief. "He's only one of the best motocross riders ever! He can do a front fender grab with Indian air and end with a no footer on a single jump."

"Wow, cool!" Vanessa bounced up and down. "What's motocross?"

I held up a hand to block her out and turned to Berkeley. "I would *love* to go, dude."

He nodded. "I'll have you added to the guest list."

He hurried to catch up with his friends, and I turned to Vanessa with a huge smile.

"I get to meet Adrenaline Dennis!" I pumped the air with my fist.

She clapped. "I still have no idea what moto-cross is!"

"Oh, sorry," I said. "Motorcycle racing. All those other things I mentioned were different tricks."

"Neat!" She gave me a thumbs-up. "And thanks for helping me stick up for Gil earlier."

I checked the area and stepped closer. "I wasn't sticking up for him, actually. I was doing it for myself."

"Oh, right. Because of your . . ." She lifted an imaginary skirt hem and started high kicking.

I sighed. "We don't dance like that, but yes."

She shook her head. "I don't know why you're keeping this a big secret. I mean, you're dancing in some Christmas show. Everyone's going to find out."

"I'm not dancing in just any Christmas show," I corrected her. "I'm performing for Christmas Around the World at the Museum of Science and Industry in Chicago! And I promise you, nobody from our school is going to go. It would mean expressing an interest in culture."

Vanessa stuck her tongue out. "You know what? The Three Musketeers were *going* to go, but now we won't."

The Three Musketeers were what she, Brooke, and Heather called themselves. They've been best friends since kindergarten. Now that Gus was gone, I envied that. The longest other friendship I've had is with Gabby, but she's not exactly one of the guys. Even if I draw a mustache on her, she's still a girl . . . just an angrier one.

"Well, thank you for the support," I told V, "but I'd rather not have the three of you giggling in the front row."

"We wouldn't!" she said, looking insulted. Then she stared into space and giggled.

I sighed. "You're thinking about me dancing, aren't you?"

She stifled her laughter behind a hand. "No. I was thinking about . . . um . . . motocross."

A girl from our class walked toward us. "Hey, Mr. E says the Polynesians settled Hawaii faster than you two can cross a room."

"Sorry," I said. "We were busy picking coconuts."

"You're so funny!" The girl giggled and then ran back to the rest of the class.

Vanessa rolled her eyes and pushed me forward. "If we had coconuts, I would've knocked you over the head with one long ago."

I flashed a smile. "What can I say? I've got a way with the ladies."

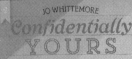